Puffin Books

Good-bye to Gumble's

'Good-bye to the Jungl
Kevin's cousin Harold
were all of them – Uncl
Harold and Jean – leav
brand-new house on a new estate.

And perhaps it would be a brand-new life too! Perhaps Walter and Doris would really reform now they had a new house and new neighbours, perhaps Kevin and Sandra wouldn't have to go on taking care of the younger ones, perhaps they would have a neat home and a nice garden like everyone else, and never worry any more about how to pay the rent or buy the food.

But all things don't come right by themselves. First there was Jean hiding on the day of the move because Walter wouldn't let her take the ugly old cat she loved so much, then Harold stealing money so that he could hand out sweets to the children at Westwood, and Doris getting so inspired by the new house that she ordered a lot of shiny new furniture which they couldn't possibly pay for. Worst of all, there was lazy, extravagant Walter, who lost his job for bad time-keeping, and seemed to be up to something shady again. Was it to be the same old story of the police and chilly, suspicious neighbours all over again?

One way and another, the young Thompsons had plenty of troubles to contend with. Yet this sequel to John Rowe Townsend's *Gumble's Yard* is an encouraging story, because of the determination of Kevin and Sandra, the two who have to bear the brunt of Walter's irresponsibility. Thanks to their own efforts, they and Harold and Jean will be all right in the end.

Good-bye to Gumble's Yard was originally published as *Widdershins Crescent*, and a number of revisions have been specially made by the author for this new Puffin edition.

John Rowe Townsend

Good-bye to Gumble's Yard

Puffin Books

Puffin Books, Penguin Books Ltd, Harmondsworth, Middlesex, England
Penguin Books, 625 Madison Avenue, New York, New York 10022, U.S.A.
Penguin Books Australia Ltd, Ringwood, Victoria, Australia
Penguin Books Canada Ltd, 2801 John Street, Markham, Ontario, Canada L3R 1B4
Penguin Books (N.Z.) Ltd, 182-190 Wairau Road, Auckland 10, New Zealand

First published by Hutchinson as *Widdershins Crescent* 1965
Published in Puffin Books under that title 1970
This revised edition first published in Puffin Books 1981

Copyright © John Rowe Townsend, 1965, 1981
All rights reserved

Set, printed and bound in Great Britain by
Cox & Wyman Ltd, Reading
Filmset in Linotype Times

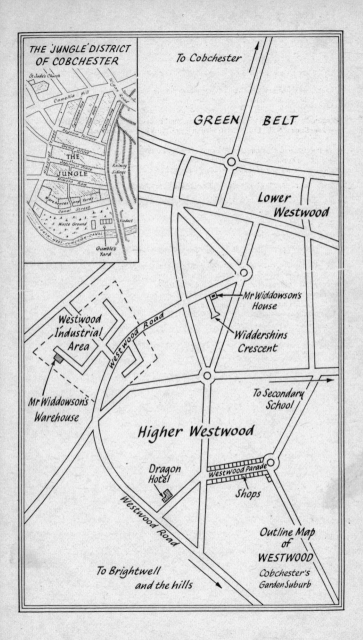

THE 'JUNGLE' DISTRICT
OF COBCHESTER

St Jude's Church
Camellia Hill
Acacia Ave
Laburnam Gdns
Worn Road
Lotus Road
Canna Road
Regent Terrace
Orchis Grove
THE
JUNGLE
Clematis Place
Mimosa Row
Warehouses and Yards
Canal Street
Waste Ground
NORTH-WEST-JUNCTION-CANAL
Railway
Sidings
Viaduct
Gumble's
Yard

To Cobchester

GREEN   BELT

Lower
Westwood

Mr Widdowson's
House

Widdershins
Crescent

Westwood
Road

Westwood
Industrial
Area

Mr Widdowson's
Warehouse

To Secondary
School

Higher Westwood

Dragon
Hotel

Westwood Parade

Shops

Westwood
Road

To Brightwell
and the hills

Outline Map
of
WESTWOOD
Cobchester's
Garden Suburb

1

'Good-bye to the Jungle,' sang my cousin Harold, to the tune of 'Tipperary'. 'Farewell, Orchid Grove. It's a long long way across to Westwood. But that's where I'll rove.'

'If I couldn't make up anything better than that,' I said, 'I wouldn't bother.'

'Well, it rhymes,' said Harold. 'And it says what we're doing.'

'Shut up and get out of the way!' said my uncle Walter. 'Kevin, give us a hand with this washstand.'

'You're bashing it into the wall, Dad,' said Harold.

'I'm not going to start worrying about the wall now,' said Walter. He looked round sharply. 'Here, Doris! Make yourself useful for once. Sandra, bring them blankets down. Jean – where's Jean? She's big enough to help, an' all.'

'Good-bye to the Jungle,' sang Harold again. 'Farewell, Orchid Grove . . .'

It was good-bye to the Jungle all right. The Jungle was a tumbledown district of the city of Cobchester. We had lived there, at 40 Orchid Grove, for five years past. But now we were leaving, because the whole district was being pulled down under slum clearance and we were to have a new house on the Westwood Estate.

There were six of us in the family. First, there was my uncle Walter. Then there was me and my sister Sandra. I'm Kevin, and when this happened last year I was fifteen. Sandra is a year younger than I am. We went to live with Walter – our father's brother – when our parents were killed

7

in an accident. Then there were Harold and Jean, who were Walter's children and therefore our cousins. Harold is eleven and Jean is eight. And finally there was Walter's friend Doris, who came to live with us when Walter's wife left him.

Two years before the move to Westwood the family had nearly broken up, when Walter and Doris walked out on us and we four children tried to set up a home of our own in an old warehouse at Gumble's Yard, down by the canal. But that trouble was sorted out, and since then we had all held together quite well. Things hadn't been perfect, it's true. What with the quarrelling between Walter and Doris, and Walter getting into trouble over some lead that was stolen from St Jude's Church roof and not keeping any job for very long, and Doris not being much of a housekeeper, and the rent always being behind, we'd had our share of trials. But Sandra and I had done our best to look after the younger ones, and we hadn't managed too badly.

And now, after years of rumours, the Jungle was being demolished and we were on our way to Westwood. At the kerb stood a van that Jack Hedley, father of my friend Dick, had borrowed from the garage where he works. As soon as we'd loaded up the van Mr Hedley was going to drive us and our belongings over to Westwood and a new life was going to begin.

'Here, you!' said Walter to Doris. 'You was keen enough to leave this house, wasn't you? Well then, get on an' do something. You can put that chair in the van for a start.'

'I'm sittin' on it.'

'Sittin', that's all you're good for . . .'

'You seem to think you're the boss around here,' said Doris sardonically. 'Givin' orders right an' left. I can't see nobody takin' much notice, though.'

As a matter of fact the van was almost loaded. While

Walter had been telling everybody what to do, and Doris had been answering him back, and Harold had been singing and dreaming and getting in the way, Sandra and I had done the work as we usually did.

We hadn't seen Jean for a few minutes.

'Where's that kid got to?' grumbled Walter. 'We're all ready but for her.' He went to the door and shouted both ways along the street. But Jean didn't appear.

'Some of you can be getting in the back of the van while I find her,' said Walter. 'I'll go in the front with Jack.'

'You're not gettin' me in there till we're ready to go,' said Doris. She sat on the doorstep and produced a bent cigarette from her apron pocket. All but one of the houses in Orchid Grove were empty now. Windows were all broken, doors had gone for firewood, rude words and pictures were scrawled on the distempered passageways.

'Hiding in one of them houses,' said Walter, 'that's where she'll be.'

He went into the middle of the street and bawled:

'Jean! Jean! Come here or I'll warm your backside for you!'

But there was still no sign of Jean.

'What's she mean by clearing off at this time?' demanded Walter. He turned on Doris. 'You fat lump, why can't you keep an eye on her? You've not been doin' anything else that I can see.'

'She's your brat, not mine,' said Doris.

'An' you, Sandra. Didn't you see her go?'

'I can tell you what she'll be up to,' said Doris indifferently. 'She'll be lookin' for that cat.'

As soon as Doris said it we knew she was right. Jean was devoted to a filthy old tom-cat that somebody had left behind when they moved. It had no name that we knew of. Jean called it 'Pussy', but you could hardly imagine a less pussy-like creature. It was lean, fierce and battle-scarred. Nobody but Jean could get near it. But with Jean it had some strange understanding. She lavished kindness on it, and it would purr loudly and rub round her ankles.

For two or three weeks past, Jean had been announcing at intervals that she was taking Pussy to Westwood with her, and Walter had been announcing at similar intervals that she blooming well wasn't. The morning of the removal, Pussy hadn't been seen.

'Well, I told her we're not takin' that mangy beast with us,' said Walter. 'Come on, Kevin, you an' Sandra come an' look for her. She can't be far away. Not you, Harold. I don't want you gettin' lost as well. You just stay with your auntie.'

Harold pulled a face but sat down on the step near Doris, not touching her. He is a little thin fair-haired boy, very like Walter.

'Good-bye to the Jungle,' he sang once more. 'Farewell, Orchid Grove.'

'We haven't gone yet,' said Doris.

Walter and Sandra and I set out to look for Jean. There weren't many places in the district where she could be. Orchid Grove was one of the last streets to go. All around were bare sites strewn with rubble, where once there had been rows of houses and hundreds of people.

In the doorway of the last house in Orchid Grove a small dirty child was playing with a china figure of a boy eating cherries.

'You seen our Jean?' asked Walter.

The child held up the cherry boy.

'Found it next door,' she said.

'You seen our Jean?'

'Look, it's eating cherries.' The little girl pretended to pick the cherries and put them in her own mouth.

'I said, you seen our Jean?'

But the child just stared. Walter kicked the china figure out of her hand. It broke in two on the step. She picked up a piece in each hand and looked from one to the other, baffled, but she didn't cry. Walter strode on.

In Hibiscus Street, which had been the main street of the Jungle, the George Inn and a couple of shops were still standing, shored up by beams where the adjoining houses had been pulled down. Opposite, in Brazil Street, were a few more surviving houses. In one of these our friends the Hedleys lived.

Walter cast an eye on the inn door.

'They're open now,' he said. 'You two keep on lookin' for Jean, will you? She can't have gone far. I'll just nip in for a quick pint of ale.'

Sandra and I exchanged looks.

'We'd better tell Mr Hedley we're not quite ready to go,' said Sandra. 'He may be waiting for us.'

In Brazil Street you could see at once which was the Hedley's house, because the outside was painted and there were curtains in the windows and the doorstep was scoured a lovely creamy yellow. Dick's mother opened the door and beamed when she saw Sandra. She is a little thin woman, sharp-faced and sharp-tongued, but she is kind to us all and she loves Sandra like a daughter.

'Our Jean's missing,' said Sandra. 'So will you tell Mr Hedley we aren't ready to go just yet. I'll call back as soon as we find her.'

'Oh well, he'll help you look for her, I dare say,' said Mrs Hedley. 'He's just puttin' his boots on now. Dick's at work.'

Dick had left school and got an apprenticeship in a printing works.

'You can step inside,' Mrs Hedley went on. 'I won't keep you a minute. And your Jean won't come to any harm. She's got her head screwed on all right for such a little lass.'

We went into the Hedleys' house. It looked as if Mrs Hedley was spring-cleaning, but that seemed odd because

11

Brazil Street was coming down like all the rest, and the Hedleys would be moving in two or three weeks' time.

'Got to keep it shipshape, like,' explained Mrs Hedley. 'I was just washin' down the walls when you came.'

'But you know what happens when you leave,' I said. 'It'll be broken into and messed up like all the other empty houses.'

'I don't care. That's nothing to do with me. I've always kept my house nice, an' I'll keep it nice to the end. When I hand in my key I'll leave the place as neat as a new pin. After that it's no business of mine what happens.'

'She's daft about lookin' after the house,' said Mr Hedley, appearing in the doorway. He's a solid man with a shock of red hair just like his son Dick's.

'I look after *you* an' all,' said Mrs Hedley grimly. 'And you'd soon know the difference if I didn't, you an' Dick. Wouldn't they, Sandra love?'

'Yes, they would,' said Sandra quietly. She knows the difference.

'Well, now, I hear there's a technical hitch,' said Mr Hedley. 'What's gone wrong?'

'Oh, it's nothing much. Jean's missing, that's all. She'll be all right. But we thought we'd better tell you we won't be ready to go till we find her.'

'I'll come an' help you. Where's your uncle?'

'He's having a pint in the George.'

'Oh. Well, let's find her quick, then, shall we? Mrs Braithwaite at the shop might have seen her. You go an' ask. I'll keep straight on down the street.'

Mrs Braithwaite's shop was at the other side of the George. It was the sort of corner shop that sells everything, but it wasn't selling much now, because it was a corner without any street. The houses next to it had all gone.

'Have you seen our Jean, Mrs Braithwaite?' I asked.

Mrs Braithwaite must be nearly eighty. All her children

12

have gone away and she doesn't hear from any of them, except maybe a card at Christmas, so she is going a bit queer with being on her own so much.

'Nay, I've not seen your Jean,' she said. 'What'd I have seen your Jean for? Never see nobody these days. Only one customer all morning.'

We turned to go, but she kept on talking.

'And that was only a little lass for a tin of catfood.'

We were half-way through the door. Sandra turned about sharply.

'A little girl buying catfood? How big? What did she look like?'

'Eh, I don't know . . .'

'Was she a round-faced, curly-haired little girl in an old red cardigan and black plimsolls?'

'Aye, that's her.'

'Well, that's our Jean,' I said. 'I thought you knew our Jean.'

'Oh, aye, that'll be her,' said Mrs Braithwaite apologetically. 'I was thinkin' of somebody else. Eh, that was daft of me. Of course it's your Jean. I know her. She stopped an' had a talk with me. You're glad to talk to anyone when you get to my age.'

'Did she say where she was going?'

'Oh aye, she told me all sorts of stuff. She said you was all goin' to Westwood Estate today, an' she said she was takin' her cat with her, come what may.'

We exchanged looks, but Mrs Braithwaite went straight on.

'She said if she couldn't take the cat she wouldn't go. But I says to her, I says, "You can't just stay here by yourself, you know, a little lass like you. Why, they wouldn't let *me* stay, an' I'm an old woman."'

'But did she say where she was going when she left the shop?' asked Sandra patiently.

'Oh aye. She got me to open the tin for her. But let me finish. I told her, an' I'm tellin' you, it's all right for the young 'uns, but when you've lived here a lifetime, like I have, you don't take to bein' sent away . . .'

'But our Jean. Where – ?'

'I told the chap from the Town Hall, I says, "I want to keep my business," I says, "it's a bit of money to add to my pension, an' it's all I have to give me an interest in life." But he says, "It's no good, Grandma" – Grandma, he called me! – he says, "It's no good, Grandma, you couldn't pay the shop rents out at Westwood, you'll be best in the old folks' home . . ."'

'Oh, what a shame!' said Sandra. She is always full of sympathy for people. But she didn't mean to lose track of what we were doing. 'Now tell us about that little girl,' she said, 'because we've got to find her. Where did she say she was going from the shop?'

'She said she thought the cat might be in his old house, down in Mimosa Row, an' she'd go an' look for him there,' said Mrs Braithwaite. 'I know it was Mimosa Row, 'cause it was where an old auntie of mine used to live. Mind you, that was years and years ago. Things was different in them days. I remember – '

But we didn't have time to stop and talk. We made excuses and hurried away down Hibiscus Street towards Mimosa Row, catching up with Mr Hedley as we went.

In Mimosa Row two or three houses were still standing, doorless and windowless, at the end nearest the railway. As we came up to the first house we heard Jean's voice from inside. She was speaking to the cat in tender tones.

'There's a dear sweet old Pussy,' she was saying. 'Did they go away and leave their poor old Pussy? Never mind, old Pussy, you've got a mum now, after all. I'm going to be your mum, and look after you . . .'

Quietly Sandra and I crept in through the open doorway.

14

On the rubble-strewn floor of what had been the living-room a battered grey cat with scarred face and torn ear crouched over the open catfood tin. He looked up suspiciously as we entered, and when I made a slight move towards him he slunk into a corner.

'You've interrupted his dinner!' cried Jean indignantly; and then, addressing the cat in the same tender voice as before: 'Poor old Pussy, did they frighten you? Never mind, they're not going to hurt my Pussy. Now finish your meal, like a good cat.'

'Fancy buying that stuff at twenty-five pence a tin!' I remarked. 'Haven't you anything better to do with your money?'

'It was my money,' said Jean defiantly. 'A lady gave me it for an errand. I can spend it how I like. That's right, Pussy, you eat it up.'

Warily Pussy returned to the open tin and went on eating, though ready to retreat at any moment.

'Come on, folks!' called Mr Hedley from the street outside. 'Time we were on our way!'

'Pussy can't come just yet,' said Jean. 'Not till he's finished.'

'Pussy can't come at all,' I said.

'But I want him,' said Jean. 'I want him to love. That's what I want him for.'

'He'll have to be put to sleep,' I said.

Jean clenched her fists.

'I'm not going to Westwood without Pussy!' she declared. And then, softening her voice to speak to the cat: 'There, there, pet, come to your mum!'

Pussy had finished eating, and now he let Jean pick him up, though he was still eyeing the rest of us with a good deal of suspicion.

'It's no good, duck,' said Mr Hedley. 'You couldn't do with him at Westwood. Anyroad, he probably wouldn't go with you, or if he did, he wouldn't stay. Cats get attached to their own homes.'

'Of course he'd come with me!' said Jean.

Sandra hadn't spoken since we arrived at the empty house. She was in one of her thoughtful moods.

'Bring him as far as the van, anyway,' she said to Jean, 'and see what happens. But you know what your dad said last time!'

And then, turning to us, Sandra added quietly:

'Poor kid, it's quite true, she wants something to love. And we'll have plenty of problems at Westwood anyway. A cat more or less won't make much difference.'

2

'Bet you five pounds that cat won't stay with us for twenty-four hours!' said Walter.

'Done!' said Mr Hedley.

He winked. On the way back from Mimosa Row he and Sandra had worked out a strategy, and it had succeeded. Walter had been led into an argument about the habits of cats, and now his love of a bet had triumphed over his distaste for Pussy. Jean carried her pet triumphantly into the van that was to take us to Westwood.

Walter sat beside Mr Hedley at the front. Doris and the two younger children occupied the bench-seat behind them. The rest of the van was full of furniture, but Sandra and I found ourselves a perch from which we could look out of the open back.

First we drove along Hibiscus Street, then up Camellia

Hill and into the Wigan Road. 'Good-bye to the Jungle!' sang Harold for the fiftieth time as we stopped at the traffic-lights, and Walter yelled at him to shut up.

Then the van headed for the centre of Cobchester. We passed the big shops, and the Town Hall, and the city magistrates' court where Walter had had to go about that lead from the church roof. Then out we went at the other side of the city, through grimy districts that weren't quite as tumble-down as the Jungle and wouldn't be demolished for another year or two. Then through miles of suburbs, getting gradu-ally cleaner and smarter: first terraces without gardens, then superior terraces with little patches of green at the front, then rows of modern semis as neat as new pins, then big separate houses with lawns and double garages. Then a stretch of country, with an old-fashioned farmhouse bang on the edge of the main road and cows grazing under the pylons. This was the Green Belt. And then came Westwood.

'Oh, isn't it *lovely*!' said Sandra.

At fourteen, Sandra is still quite small and thin, with straight fair hair and grey eyes and a sharp but honest face. She looks young for her age, but actually I sometimes think she talks like a grown-up. Maybe it's because she's used to looking after younger children and mending clothes and always knowing where food is cheapest.

And I suppose a grown-up might think Westwood is lovely. It's full of neat lawns and pathways and shrubberies. But I think it's as dull as ditchwater, not like the old Jungle, which had all kinds of odd corners and alleyways and derelict warehouses and yards and a canal and a viaduct.

Westwood is Cobchester's overspill. It has thousands and thousands of people, and miles and miles of roads and avenues and drives and mounts and crescents, all looking exactly alike.

It took Mr Hedley quite a while to find Widdowson Crescent, where we were going to live. He stopped the van

17

two or three times to ask the way. But at last we turned from a main road into a cul-de-sac, the van drew up, and Mr Hedley came round and opened up the back. Sandra and I got down and stretched our legs, and the others came round from the front, Jean with her cat draped round her neck. And here we were outside our new house, which was No. 17.

It was well away from the main road, being just at the point where the houses started to go round in a ring. At the other side of the street, some of the houses were only half built, and men were working on them. At our side nearly all the houses were occupied, but the gardens were just wilder-nesses of mud and brickbats – all except one, and that was neat and pretty with a little square green lawn and bedding plants, like a miracle.

We looked up at our square brick house, with its bay window and its new paintwork, as respectable as any-thing.

'Oh, isn't it *lovely*!' said Sandra again.

'Lovely?' said Walter. 'Ten pounds a week rent to pay, instead of three! Two miles to the pub and twelve miles to work. Lovely?'

'It's a sight better than that hole we've come from,' said Doris.

'Well, you better not start complainin' about it, anyroad,' said Walter. 'It was you that wanted to come here, not me, an' don't you forget it.'

'We hadn't no option that I can see,' said Doris. 'We couldn't have stayed on in a tent when they pulled the house down, could we?'

'There's ways an' means,' said Walter. He put on a cunning look. 'A corporation tenancy's a valuable asset, you know that? I mean it's worth hard cash.'

'Yer daft,' said Doris.

'I'm not daft. There's ways of swapping it for a rented house back in town and cash in hand as well.' He wagged a finger at her. 'An' I can still do it if I feel like it, any time. So you watch your step.'

'An' you shut yer flipping trap,' said Doris.

Mr Hedley was getting impatient.

'Can I help you unload?' he said. 'Then I'll have to be getting back. I'm on late turn this week and the boss'll be expecting me.'

'Aye, thank you, Jack. It's her, with her natterin', that holds things up.'

It was Walter who'd been doing the talking, but nobody bothered to tell him so. With a flourish he unlocked the front door. Mr Hedley and Sandra and I began to carry our furniture up the path. A group of small children had gathered round the van, but the half-built houses were a bigger attraction than our removal, and soon they disappeared. Doris sat on the low garden wall, produced another bent cigarette from somewhere, and lit up. She is a slow, bulky woman with a flabby, expressionless face. It's hard to tell what she's thinking, or even whether she's thinking at all.

Meanwhile Walter, inside the house, issued instructions to the rest of us, and Sandra and I got on with the work, not taking much notice. It wasn't until the job was finished and Mr Hedley had set off back to the Jungle that Doris came inside. She looked first at the furniture we'd put in the living room.

'It dun't look much, does it?' she said.

I knew just what she meant. The truth was that our furniture was nothing but a few sticks. There were just enough chairs to go round, but most of them were rickety. There was a decrepit old table and a dresser with a cracked marble top and a broken-down sofa and a few other oddments, and that was all we had downstairs. Upstairs was no better. In Orchid Grove it hadn't seemed to matter, because the house was so old and poky and dirty that proper furniture would be wasted on it. But here in the nice new council house our few bits and pieces looked very poor.

'It's what you had before,' said Walter.

'Well, it won't do here,' said Doris.

'Gettin' to be quite the housewife, eh?' said Walter jeeringly. 'I never heard you say anything about furniture at Orchid Grove. You'll be wantin' carpets next, I suppose, an' tablecloths. Goin' up in the world. Maybe you think you'll have Lord an' Lady Tomnoddy droppin' in for a cup o' tea now you're in Westwood. "Can I press you to a jam tart, my lady?" Aw, come off it, can't you?'

'There'd be money to buy something decent if you stopped spendin' all your wages on beer an' horses.'

Walter flared up.

'It's nothing to do with you how I spend my wages. I earn them, don't I?'

'Yes, an' who has to feed all them kids? I do. An' they're not my kids. You ought to be ashamed, Walter Thompson–'

'Shut up or I'll clout you!' said Walter.

Doris was going to say something more, and Walter probably would have clouted her as he said, but just then Jean came in with the cat still draped round her neck.

'It's Pussy's teatime,' she said.

Walter swivelled round and shook his fist at Jean instead.

'Pussy's flippin' teatime!' he bawled. 'Take that flippin' animal out of here or I'll knock its flippin' head off, an' yours too!'

Jean was unmoved.

'There, Pussy, take no notice of him,' she said. 'I'll find you something in a minute.'

Walter half rose. Jean walked out with dignity, though she would have moved fast enough if Walter had really gone for her. She reached the door in time to open it for a caller. There was a young woman there with a tray in her hands and a little boy standing beside her.

20

'I thought you might like a cup o' tea,' she said timidly.

She had a round, pretty face with dark hair and big eyes. Walter looked her up and down. Then he smiled. It was the first time he'd smiled that day.

'Why, come in, Mrs . . .?'

'Robbins. I live next door.'

'Come in, Mrs Robbins. Now that's right kind of you. Isn't it, Doris love?'

Doris said nothing. Mrs Robbins advanced to the table and put her tray down.

'I brought five cups,' she said. 'Is that right? I thought maybe you wouldn't have had time to unpack your pots, like.'

'That's just right, Mrs Robbins,' said Walter. He smiled at her again. 'You was very thoughtful.' He waved her to the rickety sofa. 'Sit down, Mrs Robbins. Is that your little lad? Let's see, he must be five or six, eh?'

'He's seven,' said Mrs Robbins. 'Seven last week.'

'Get away!' said Walter in a tone of extreme surprise. 'I wouldn't have thought you was old enough to have a lad of seven.'

Mrs Robbins blushed.

'What's his name?' asked Walter. 'He's like you, isn't he?'

'Most folks say he's like his dad,' said Mrs Robbins. 'Leslie, that's his name.' She sat on the edge of the sofa and looked round her uneasily.

'Come on, Sandra, pass them cups round,' said Walter. 'Sandra's my niece, Mrs Robbins. A great help to all of us. Isn't she, Doris love?'

Doris scowled and still said nothing. Walter sat on the sofa beside Mrs Robbins and put his head rather close to hers. She recoiled a little.

'I hope we'll be very happy neighbours,' he said. He raised his cup as if it was a glass. 'To our closer acquaintanceship, Mrs Robbins.'

Mrs Robbins didn't look too happy. She glanced at Walter doubtfully. Of course, he would have looked better if he'd shaved that day.

Walter seemed to think he was making quite a hit.

'I expect we'll see a lot more of each other,' he said, and drained his cup.

'Aw, turn it in, Walter Thompson, can't you?' snarled Doris suddenly. 'Who d'you think you are? Paul Newman?'

Mrs Robbins shot a startled look at Doris and started to get up.

'You're not impressin' her, you know,' said Doris, still addressing Walter. 'She's got a husband an' a proper home, not like this. Don't make a bigger fool of yourself than you are.'

Mrs Robbins, alarmed, was gathering the cups on to her tea-tray.

'That's right, love,' said Doris grimly. 'Hop it. You seen all you came to see, haven't you? You don't need to see no more.'

'I – I never came to see nothin',' stammered Mrs Robbins. 'I just thought you might be glad of a cup o' tea.' She took Leslie's hand and made for the door. Doris followed, and called after her down the garden path:

'Tell 'em all what we're like! Save 'em the trouble o' findin' out!'

Walter raised his fist as Doris turned back into the room.

'You great fat lump!' he snapped. 'Showin' us up in the first five minutes!'

'She'd have found out soon enough!' said Doris.

But Doris looked far from triumphant.

'You needn't think I enjoy it,' she went on bitterly. 'If you want to know, I wish I was like her, well dressed and a proper hair-do, and her little boy dressed lovely, an' there she is, all set to go callin' on neighbours an' takin' cups o' tea an' so on. An' then her husband comes home. Brings her flowers, I wouldn't wonder. That's the sort o' life I could do with, but I'll never get it with you!'

Walter was white with rage.

'Get out, you kids!' he yelled. 'What d'you think a garden's for? Go out into it! An' as for you . . .'

He turned to Doris again. I wondered if he was going to hit her. If he didn't do it in the next minute or two he probably wouldn't.

'Come on, Kevin,' said Sandra quietly. We went out and sat on the low brick wall. The sound of voices floated out to us. It was a pretty violent row this time. Harold appeared, filthy dirty because he'd been exploring the building site, but Sandra didn't tell him off. A minute later, along came Jean with the cat, and all four of us sat in a row on the wall, saying nothing. The two younger ones grinned a bit when they heard swear-words coming out of the house. They were quite used to quarrels, and took it all in their stride.

'I'll go in and get us some tea when they calm down,' said Sandra. 'I know there's food in the kitchen, I saw to it myself.'

'P'raps they'll make up and go round to the pub,' suggested Harold.

'It's two miles to the pub,' I said.

Sandra grimaced.

'I never thought I'd be sorry there isn't a pub near by,' she said. 'But it had its points in Orchid Grove, when they could just nip round to the George and leave us in peace for a bit.'

'You know what, Sandra?' I said. 'I think we'll have a rough time here to start with. But maybe things will get better when we settle down.'

'I hope so,' said Sandra. She was silent for quite a while.

The cat rubbed himself round Jean's legs, purring.

'It's Pussy's teatime,' said Jean for the second time. 'Sandra, he's hungry. He won't get rats and mice to eat here, like in the Jungle.'

'I'll find something for him,' said Sandra. 'In a minute. When they've finished.'

We four were silent. Noises from the house showed that the row was taking its course. Doris was heading for sobs, and Walter had taken on a note of injured innocence.

'Ten minutes more,' said Sandra expertly, 'and it'll all be over.'

3

I heard the alarm-clock ring in the front bedroom. I heard Walter swear at it. Then there was silence.

I was uneasy. I knew the household ought to be stirring. But I was sleepy, too. I dozed off again, to be wakened by Sandra, who was shaking me.

'Come on, lazybones,' she said. 'Quarter to eight. School bus goes at twenty past.'

That was a drawback to Widdowson Crescent. The school at this side of Westwood Estate was still not built, and we had to go early each morning by special bus to a school some miles away that was taking the children from our district for the time being.

'Is *he* up?' I asked, meaning Walter.

Sandra pulled a face.

'No,' she said. 'I've tried twice to get him up, but it wasn't any good. You try, Kevin. Tell him his breakfast's ready.'

I knew Walter was supposed to start work at eight o'clock at Vincent's engineering works, where he was a labourer. And Vincent's, like our school, was a long bus ride away.

'He can't make it now,' I said.

'He could find some excuse,' said Sandra. 'Better to be late than lose another day's pay.'

We had been in Widdowson Crescent for a fortnight, and in the second week Walter had twice taken a day off work because he couldn't get up in time.

I didn't like it but I knew I ought to try. So I went into the front bedroom. Walter was snoring gently. His wispy fair hair was beginning to go grey, I noticed. He'd shaved a day or two ago, but his chin was stubbly. Seeing him asleep I thought, as I always did, how like Harold he was. Whenever I got fed up with Walter (which was pretty often) I used to remind myself that he was fond of Harold. That was his redeeming feature. Otherwise not even his best friends, if he had any, could have said that Walter was a specially nice character.

And Harold, being as loyal as they come, was devoted to his dad.

I shook Walter, gently at first, then more vigorously. He opened his eyes. They are just the same bluey-grey as Harold's.

'Clear off!' he said, and turned over.

I shook him again.

'You're late for work,' I said.

'Leave me alone. What's it to do with you?'

'Well, the rent's to be paid on Monday,' I said. This was what Sandra and I were worrying about.

'Mind yer own business,' said Walter. But all the same he pulled himself far enough up to rest an elbow on the pillow. He was wearing the shirt he'd been wearing for the past few days, and it wasn't too clean.

'Pass me them fags, Kevin. On the mantelpiece. And me lighter.'

I handed Walter the cigarette packet. There was only one left. He took it out, lit it with the big ugly lighter he'd made for himself one time when he had a job at a Royal Ordnance Factory, and dropped the packet on the floor.

25

'What time is it, Kevin?'

'About ten to eight,' I said.

'Aw, it's too late, even if I felt like goin'. An' I don't. Not so well this mornin'. A bit tired, like.' He drew on his cigarette and tipped ash over the edge of the bed.

'Has Sandra made some breakfast?'

'She's making it now.'

'Tell her to bring me a cup o' tea an' some bread an' drippin'. No need to bring anything for *her*.' He indicated the sleeping form of Doris, who was no more than a shape under the bedclothes.

'You're not going to work, then?'

'You heard,' said Walter. He blew out smoke. 'Tell Sandra three spoons o' sugar. An' get a move on, lad. When I was your age I didn't hang about like you do.'

I took Walter his tea and bread-and-dripping, and closed the door. Sandra helped Jean to finish dressing herself, then gave us all our breakfasts, the same as Walter's. There were some fish-heads for Pussy that she'd scrounged at the fishmonger's on the Parade. Pussy was still with us, and Jean was more devoted to him than ever, though he showed little sign of being friendly with the rest of us. Walter had lost his five-pound bet with Mr Hedley that Pussy wouldn't stay, but he hadn't paid up yet and he didn't like to be reminded about it. For the moment the cat was tolerated, and was all right as long as he remembered to keep out of the way of Walter's boot.

After breakfast I cleaned up a bit with an old broom while Sandra washed the pots. And at ten past eight, in good time for the school bus, the four of us were ready. There was still no sign of life from Walter or Doris.

It was a lovely clear pale-blue morning in late April. In the spinney behind the half-built houses, the trees were all coming into leaf. Red and orange wallflowers glowed in the neat garden of No. 11. At No. 9 the washing had been done early, and white clothes on the line billowed in the breeze like sails. As we passed No. 5 a boy and girl came out, making for the school bus like us. I knew their names. They were Donald and Margaret Bates. I waved to them. But as they reached the garden gate their mother called them back, and kept them waiting until we'd gone past.

'You know why that is?' said Sandra to me. 'That's so they don't walk with us.'

'What's wrong with us?' I said. 'We haven't done them any harm.'

Sandra didn't answer for a moment. Then she asked:

'How long have you had that jacket, Kevin?'

'A year or two,' I said. I looked down at it. It was getting short in the sleeves, and frayed as well.

'You had it when we were at Gumble's Yard,' said Sandra. 'It came from the bring-and-buy sale at St Jude's, three years ago, and I can't mend it any more.'

'Well, clothes don't matter all that much,' I said.

'They matter to some,' said Sandra. 'And it's not so much the clothes as what they stand for. It's – oh, Kevin, it's *them*.'

I knew what she meant. Walter and Doris. A family with Walter and Doris at the head of it is an undesirable family, naturally. But I wasn't as worried as Sandra. Besides, I was used to the situation. Even in the Jungle there were people who looked askance at us. Maybe we were a bit more noticeable here at Westwood, that was all.

'Good-bye to the Jungle – ' began Harold.

'Oh, shut up!' said Sandra irritably. Then:

'You know what, Kevin? I always had my doubts. Well, I don't like it here. I mean, I like Westwood but I think we're worse off here than we were in the Jungle.'

'Oh, I like it,' I said. 'And it's healthy. Look at Harold's cheeks.'

Harold had spent most of his spare time in the last

fortnight playing in the building site. He certainly looked pink-cheeked and fit.

'I like it here, too,' said Harold comfortably. 'And I like school. You can slide in the corridors, they're so shiny.'

We were passing a big house, surrounded by garden, at the corner of our street and Westwood Road. Sandra nudged me.

'That's Alderman Widdowson's house,' she said.

'Widdowson!' I said. 'Same name as the street!'

'That's right,' said Sandra, who is always well informed on these matters. 'They called the street after him because it was built alongside his house and he'd been on the council for years and years and been chairman of the housing committee and all kinds of things.'

'Fancy having a street named after you!' I said.

'When I'm famous,' said Harold, 'I'll have a street named after *me*. Not just a little street like this. A great big road. Thompson Motorway. Named after Sir Harold Thompson, the well-known scientist.'

'That'll be the day,' said Sandra dryly.

Harold is apt to be carried away by his own daydreams.

'There he is!' said Sandra after a minute. 'Alderman Widdowson. Old Widdershins, they call him.'

'Like the street again,' I said. 'Most people seem to call it Widdershins Crescent. He doesn't really look all that old though, does he?'

From the Westwood Road bus stop, where we waited for the school bus, we had a good view into Mr Widdowson's garden. Mr Widdowson, now opening his garage door, was a tallish, thickset gentleman wearing a heavy dark overcoat. He had a rather large pale oval face and horn-rimmed spectacles. I guessed he was about fifty years old.

'He owns that big furniture shop down on Westwood Parade,' said Sandra, still full of information. 'And about a dozen others, all over Cobchester. Look, that must be his boy and girl getting into the car now. Don't they look alike – both so dark and curly? They must be about our age. David and Anne, that's what their names are.'

'I'm surprised you don't know their birthdays,' I said sarcastically, 'and what they had for breakfast.'

Sandra was unmoved.

'If it was left to you we wouldn't know much, would we?' she said. 'Well, I bet their father's taking them to school. David goes to Cobchester College, and Anne goes to Cobchester Girls' College. It's the same place really – one's the boys' school and one's the girls' school.'

'*I* might go to Cobchester College,' said Harold casually.

We thought this was just Harold imagining things, and we didn't take any notice. But a moment later he said it again.

Sandra and I rounded on him.

'*You* go to Cobchester College?' I said.

'Don't be so daft, Harold,' said Sandra. 'It's ever so posh.'

Cobchester College is about the best-known day school in England. They go to Oxford and Cambridge from there.

'Well, I might,' said Harold. 'Mr Welling told me so. That's my new teacher. He said they have a special exam in a few weeks' time, and I ought to go in for it. Anybody can go there for nothing if they pass the exam.'

'And how many pass it?' I asked.

'Oh, about a dozen, I think.'

'And how many go in for it?'

'He said over a thousand.'

'Then what chance do you think *you've* got?' I demanded.

'Oh, I expect I'd get it,' said Harold calmly. 'I'm one of the clever ones, you know. Everybody says so.'

'You can't be all *that* clever,' I said unbelievingly.

'Of course he can,' said Sandra, rallying round him. 'He's the cleverest boy in Westwood.' She looked across at the other dozen or so children who were also waiting for the school bus but keeping their distance from us.

'You'll show them, won't you, duck?' she said. 'There's none of them any good compared with our Harold.'

I looked down at Harold – a little, thin, fair-haired boy with knobbly knees. He was wearing a fawn jersey that had once been mine, a pair of patched and faded jeans, and grubby plimsolls. I thought of the Cobchester College boys I'd seen around, so well dressed and well spoken. The contrast was too much.

'He'll never go there,' I said. 'What, one of our family at Cobchester College? Have a bit of sense, Sandra.'

Sandra put her arm around Harold's shoulders.

'He can go anywhere, can Harold,' she said. 'Nobody's going to do him out of anything.'

She spoke with immense determination. It might have been his mother talking, if he'd had a mother.

The school bus swept round the corner. There was a rush for the platform. Harold and Jean were on first, and got seats; we saw to that.

4

'Nip along to the Parade, Sandra,' said Doris, 'an' get me five pound of potaters and a two-pound jar of plum jam and a quarter of tea.'

It was Saturday morning.

'All right,' said Sandra. 'Give me the money.'

'They can put it on the slate.'

'Well, they won't,' said Sandra. 'Not at Johnson's, nor at Lennard's. Not till you've paid something off.'

'Go the other way along Westwood Road, then,'

said Doris. 'There's some more shops up by the bus terminus.'

'I'll still need money,' said Sandra.

Doris glowered but climbed up on a chair arm and reached a jam-jar from the top shelf of the cupboard. From it she extracted a much-crumpled five-pound note.

'You know what that is?' she said grimly. 'That's part of the rent money. Still, we've got to have something to eat, haven't we?'

Sandra and I exchanged glances.

'It's no good lookin' like that,' said Doris. 'It's your uncle. Two days off this week, so he only drew thirty pounds, an' lucky not to get the sack. Then he has to put five pounds on a horse, an' it loses of course. And then he has to spend all last night down at the Dragon.'

'You were with him, weren't you?' said Sandra coldly.

'Shut yer flippin' trap,' said Doris. She aimed a half-hearted swipe at Sandra's head. Then she sat down heavily at the kitchen table. The chair creaked under her.

'If you want to know,' she said, 'I'm fed up with all this. Fed up to the back teeth. Years of it in the other place, an' it's just the same here. Struggling on with all four of you, an' never enough money. It disheartens me.'

She was silent for a moment, then went on:

'Look at all this junk we've got here. Call it furniture? It's only fit for firewood. You should see the stuff they're selling at Widdowson's shop, down on the Parade. Lovely. An' everybody else in the street can have it, but not us . . .'

The furniture seemed to be on Doris's mind. She had mentioned it two or three times in the past few weeks.

'Oh, come on, Kevin,' said Sandra. 'Let's go down to the shops.' And when we were outside she went on: 'I'm sick of hearing her, always sorry for herself.'

But I was still thinking about Doris and the furniture.

'You know what?' I said. 'Doris is changing.'

31

'Well, if she did it could only be for the better,' said Sandra bitterly, 'but I haven't noticed any sign.'

'Still, she *is* changing,' I said. 'A year or two ago she wouldn't have been going on about furniture. She didn't care.'

'It wasn't worth caring in the Jungle,' said Sandra.

'But she wanted to leave the Jungle,' I said. 'Walter didn't, but she did. See what I mean? She's getting tired of living like this.'

'Then why doesn't she do something about it? Such as keeping the house clean? If you and I didn't clean it a bit each day it'd be as bad as the old one by now.'

'Well, you know what she is,' I said. 'It takes a lot to get her moving. But remember, when Mrs Robbins came in from next door, Doris was jealous about her clothes and her hair-do and her little boy being so well turned out?' I was warming to the theme. 'I'll tell you what it is, Sandra. I reckon now she's getting older she'd like to be more respectable. And coming here to Westwood where everything's clean and neat has brought it on more strongly. She never wanted to be like all the other women before, but now she does.'

'Some hope!' said Sandra.

Now the great idea struck me.

'Sandra!' I said eagerly. 'Remember Batten's junkshop on Camellia Hill? They had lots and lots of furniture, very cheap, that people didn't want to take with them when they moved. Some of it looked all right. Well, if we picked it carefully we could get everything we need for a few pounds to make the house decent.'

Sandra stopped in her tracks. She didn't show enthusiasm; that isn't Sandra's way. But I could tell she was impressed. I added:

'Maybe that would encourage Doris to make a fresh start. And we could do with a fresh start. Why, Harold might win that scholarship to Cobchester College. He needs a proper home. So does Jean. We all do.'

'Where would we get a few pounds?' asked Sandra.

That was a fair question, and I didn't know the answer.

'We'd have to sell something,' I said uncertainly.

'And what have we got to sell?'

'Well . . . I don't know. Perhaps we could earn something. We made some money from selling firewood once.'

'It'd take years before we made enough,' said Sandra.

I wasn't disheartened by her objections. They were proof that she was taking my idea seriously.

'We could ask the Cruelty,' I suggested. (That's the N.S.P.C.C.) 'They often help people to get things they need.'

'Begging!' said Sandra, disgusted.

'It isn't begging if it's things you've got to have.'

'Of course it's begging. And I won't do it.'

'Well, then . . .' I said.

I looked at Sandra and then at our wrists. I knew what it was coming to.

'The watches,' I said.

Sandra had a little gold wrist watch and I had a big masculine-looking chrome one on a flexible strap. These watches were very special. We had been given them two years earlier, after the affair at Gumble's Yard, as a reward for helping to get back some stolen property. Our friend Dick Hedley had one, too.

'They must be worth quite a lot,' said Sandra.

I felt slightly sickened at the thought of getting money for the watches. They were our most prized possessions. In fact they were our only possessions of any value, and we'd had no end of a job keeping them out of Walter's hands all this time.

'Where would we sell them?' I asked.

'Perhaps we wouldn't actually need to sell them. Perhaps we could pawn them.'

'No, that's no good,' I said. I knew about pawning things. 'You have to pay the money back and a good deal of interest as well. We'd never get them back, so we might as well sell them and be done with it.'

'I expect we could sell them at a jeweller's,' said Sandra.

I wasn't too sure. I imagined them asking a lot of questions. I also imagined them diddling us. And then I had another brainwave.

'We've got to go to the Jungle anyway if we want to buy the furniture,' I said, 'so let's ask Mr Hedley to help us sell them. He'll know what to do.'

Sandra brightened. As it was Saturday, Dick Hedley would be at home, and Sandra is always glad to see Dick.

I knew I had won.

'Hurry up and buy those spuds,' I said, 'We'll go straight after dinner.'

We had arrived at the parade of shops, and Sandra was already inspecting the greengrocery.

'Fifty pence for five pounds of rotten old potatoes like those,' she commented. 'It's robbery. I've a good mind to go to the other lot of shops after all.'

'Not today,' I said hastily. The other shops were a mile away. 'Not today!'

'You're not going to sell those watches!' said Mr Hedley.

'We are.'

'Oh no, you're not. Do you think I'd let Dick sell his?'

'He doesn't need to.'

'Well, neither do you.'

'But we've just told you,' I said patiently, 'we need some money to buy furniture at Batten's for our new house . . .'

'I know, I know,' said Mr Hedley. 'And I'm just telling you, you don't need to sell your watches. I'll lend you the money.'

'That's no good,' said Sandra. 'We couldn't pay you back. So it would be just the same as giving us it.'

34

'Oh no it won't,' said Mr Hedley. 'You can give me a solemn promise to pay it back when you're earning. I can wait a year or two.'

'A solemn promise in writing!' added his son Dick with sudden enthusiasm. 'A deed!'

Dick is our best and oldest friend. He is a big, red-haired boy, full of life and brimming with ideas, and he is always ready to help anybody if he can. The only thing wrong with Dick is that he's bossy.

I liked the idea of a deed myself. It made it all seem all right and not scrounging, and it was an important grown-up way of doing things.

Dick brought a sheet of cartridge-paper. He and I wrote out the deed together. Mr Hedley grinned and shrugged his shoulders. He wasn't bothered about deeds. But it was a good one. It began with 'Whereas', because deeds always do.

Whereas, on this second day of May 1981, we, Sandra and Kevin Thompson, have borrowed the sum of Forty Pounds from John Hedley, receipt of which is hereby acknowledged,

Now this deed witnesseth that we, the said Sandra and Kevin Thompson, undertake that on the improvement of our financial position we will repay the said Forty Pounds to the said John Hedley, so help us God.

Given under our own hands this second day of May 1981:

Kevin Thompson
Sandra Thompson

Dick read it over with satisfaction.

'That's fine,' he said. 'Very good security.' He added at the foot of the document:

In the presence of the undersigned as witness: Richard Hedley.

We handed the deed to Mr Hedley, and he counted four ten-pound notes into Sandra's hand.

'You go and choose what you want,' he said. 'I'll bring the van round to Batten's in an hour's time and we'll take the stuff straight over to Westwood today. I'll be busy with my own removal next week.'

Dick and I spent a few minutes aiming stones at the headless stump of a lamp-post while Sandra paid a visit to old Mrs Braithwaite at the shop next to the George. The Jungle was almost deserted now. More houses had been pulled down in the few weeks since we left Orchid Grove. And as the district was cleared it had begun to look quite different. You could now see that it was actually a hillside, sloping down towards the canal. Some time in the past there must even have been grass on it.

There were other odd things about these last days of the Jungle. You could now see the whole pattern where the streets had been. It all looked different and much smaller. And what had once been quite a walk round the houses – say from the middle of Orchid Grove to the middle of Begonia Terrace – was now just a few strides across an empty site.

Here and there were old possessions that people had simply abandoned, because they weren't worth taking to Westwood and they wouldn't fetch anything at the junkshop. A very old man, with a pram that looked just about as old, was rooting among the debris. Dick and I examined a decrepit sofa covered in brown leathercloth, and wondered whether it would be worth retrieving, but Sandra, when she joined us after her visit to Mrs Braithwaite, rejected it on sight.

'Full of moth,' she said briefly.

So off we went to Batten's shop on Camellia Hill. The district at the other side of the Hill is St Jude's, where our friend Tony Boyd used to be curate. It is not due to come down for another year or two. But the Camellia Hill shops all look decrepit and don't seem to do much business.

Batten's is a big, dirty old shop that hasn't been painted for donkeys' years and will never be painted again. It doesn't sell anything but junk. It has old gloomy pictures and cracked mirrors and brass fenders and tin baths. You wouldn't think anyone could possibly make a living out of it. In fact nobody knows how old Nick Batten *does* make a living from it.

He came shambling from the back when we entered: a tall, bent figure in a frayed grey suit. He wore a hearing aid.

'You have a lot of furniture that people didn't want to take with them to the new estate, haven't you?' said Dick.

Mr Batten looked sharply at him and adjusted the hearing aid.

'Furniture from demolished houses!' said Dick in a louder voice.

'I don't want no more,' said Mr Batten. He spoke loudly, as deaf people sometimes do.

'We don't want to sell it,' Dick explained. 'We want to buy it.'

Mr Batten didn't hear the explanation.

'There's no market for it,' he said. 'I can't get rid of the stuff.'

'But we're not trying to sell any!'

'You might as well chop it up and burn it,' said Mr Batten.

This time Dick bawled into his ear:

'We want to *buy* some!'

Mr Batten heard this and was surprised. He looked at each of us in turn.

'Who's it for?' he asked.

'It's for my uncle,' I said, 'over at Westwood.'

'I can't deliver out to Westwood,' said Mr Batten with an air of finality.

'We don't need it delivered,' said Dick patiently. 'My dad'll come for it with a van.'

'You what?'

'Oh gosh!' said Dick to me in a low voice. 'You'd never think he was here to do business, would you!'

Mr Batten couldn't hear that remark, but he guessed it was impolite.

'Don't stand there mutterin',' he said.

Sandra stood on tiptoe and almost shrieked at him:

'We want to buy some furniture, and we've a van coming to take it away!'

Reluctantly Mr Batten nodded.

'Aye, well, I suppose I'd better let you have something,' he said. 'Don't be too long about it. Look round an' see if there's anything you want. It's none of it so brilliant, I can tell you.'

We burrowed among the stacks of junk. Everything was covered with dust, which settled on our faces and clothes and made us cough. Chairs, tables and cupboards were piled high on each other. Some were cracked or splintered, some had legs loose or missing. We worked out a system by which Dick and I sorted out item after item and Sandra gave the verdict on each. There was some quite solid stuff among the rubbish. Sandra had brought a shopping-list, and the pile of things we'd chosen grew steadily as she ticked the items off.

After a while Sandra announced that we'd got what we needed, and the only question was whether we could afford it. Some of the items had prices chalked on them – never more than a few pounds – but others gave no indication. Mr Batten turned each of these over, squinted at it without enthusiasm, and thought of a figure, apparently at random. One piece, a chest of drawers, aroused his particular scorn.

'I'll give you that for nothing!' he said. 'Neither good workmanship nor good materials. When I was a lad they made 'em in solid mahogany an inch thick, an' they could work it, too. Just look at that wood – not fit for orange-boxes. I'd be robbin' you if I was to charge you ten pence for it. Now, let's add up what you owe me. Two pounds fifty and one pound fifty for them two chairs, that's three pounds, and another four pounds fifty for that table, seven pounds fifty, say seven pounds. And one pound fifty for each of them four whatsits over there, say another fiver. That's eleven pounds altogether . . .'

He added it all up, dropping a pound or two at every stage, and the total came to thirty-two pounds.

'You could buy a carpet as well,' Dick suggested.

'A carpet!' echoed Sandra. Her eyes shone. We had never had a carpet.

There was a rolled carpet leaning against a wall, and Mr Batten unrolled it on the floor for us. It had a floral pattern in pink and beige, and was a bit faded but not threadbare.

'It's lovely!' said Sandra. 'Isn't it lovely, Dick? A real carpet! How much is it, Mr Batten?'

Mr Batten looked at the back of the carpet.

'Twelve pound, that one,' he said.

Sandra's face fell.

'Not worth it, though,' Mr Batten went on. 'I gave too much for it in the first place. Let's say ten pound.'

That was still too much. Dick shouted in Mr Batten's ear:

'We've only got forty pounds altogether!'

'Aye, well, let's see – thirty-two plus ten: that's forty, near enough.'

Sandra handed over the money. We started moving our purchases out on to the pavement, so as not to keep Mr Hedley waiting when he came with the van. When we'd finished, Mr Batten came and looked at the heap. He shook his head.

'Nay,' he said, 'it's not worth forty pound, that lot. You should have seen the stuff my mother had, back in the nineteen-twenties. That was *real* furniture, that was. Here, take this.'

He pushed a five-pound note back into Sandra's hand.

5

Once again we sat in the back of Mr Hedley's van, driving out to Westwood with a load of furniture. Dick and Sandra were as pleased as Punch, almost as if they'd been setting up house themselves. And Sandra had a five-pound note in her handbag, because Mr Hedley wouldn't take back the money that Mr Batten had refunded to us.

'You hang on to it, love,' he told Sandra. 'It'll come in handy one of these days.'

Sandra hummed a little tune, and shot happy glances at me and the Hedleys and the furniture.

'It's just right!' she said with satisfaction. 'It's just right! If it was any worse it wouldn't be worth having, and if it was any better Walter'd sell it next time he was hard up.'

I felt happy just because of Sandra's happiness. She was unusually talkative, too.

'You wait till I've polished it all up a bit,' she went on. 'We'll have a proper home, just like anybody else.'

'And a carpet in the sitting-room!' added Dick.

Sandra's eyes shone again at the thought of the carpet.

The van turned into Widdowson Crescent. The usual little crowd of children appeared as it drew up in front of No. 17, but they soon vanished when they saw it was somebody they knew.

'I know what we'll do,' said Dick. 'My dad wants to get home as soon as we can. So let's put all the stuff outside the front door, and then when Dad and I have gone you can ring the bell and give your auntie a surprise.'

I didn't bother to tell Dick that we didn't give people surprises in our household. Surprises just seemed to come unasked. But I thought it would be quite a good thing for him and his father to be out of the way before Doris saw what we'd done, because you couldn't be quite sure how she would react. She might have seen fit to tell Mr Hedley off for sticking his nose into her affairs. So we arranged the furniture from Batten's in front of the house, giving each piece a wipe with a cloth to get some of the dust off it. And then Mr Hedley and Dick drove off in the van and I rang the front-door bell.

It was a surprise to hear the click of heels instead of the usual shuffle of down-at-heel slippers as Doris came to the door. She was dressed up, just as if she'd been ready to go round to the Dragon. For Doris to be all dressed up by four o'clock in the afternoon was unusual. And her expression seemed livelier than usual.

'Hullo!' she said. 'I wondered where you'd been. Come in an' look . . .'

Then her eyes popped as she noticed the furniture.

We'd expected her to be surprised. But we hadn't thought she'd be quite so startled as she was.

'What's all that?' she demanded.

'We got it from Batten's,' said Sandra proudly. 'It's for the house. You kept saying how short of things we were. Well, now we've got everything we need.'

Doris's eyes grew wider still.

'You got all that stuff from Batten's?'

'Yes, we did. Aren't you pleased?'

'Come in here,' said Doris faintly. 'Foller me. Into the sittin'-room. There now.'

We were as staggered as Doris had been a minute earlier. For the room was crammed full of shiny new furniture.

'Eh, two lots of furniture within an hour!' said Doris. 'You took my breath away just now, I can tell you.' She sat

41

down heavily in one of the new chairs. 'Aye, well, I suppose you meant it for the best, but we don't want Batten's old junk now, do we?'

'Where did this come from?' asked Sandra suspiciously.

'It's from Widdowson's store, down on Westwood Parade. Lovely, isn't it?' A gleam of pride was kindling in Doris's eye as she got over the shock of a moment ago. 'Pass me that duster, Sandra. There, look, you can see your face in the table top.'

'How much did it all cost?'

'Eh, I don't remember. Let's see. Three pound a week for the dining set, and two for the three-piece suite, an' one fifty for the bed. You work it out, I can't.'

'But what will it cost altogether?' asked Sandra. 'The price, I mean, not the weekly payments.'

'I never asked,' said Doris.

'It's lovely, isn't it?' I said admiringly.

But Sandra's face was setting into the thin-lipped line that always reminds me of our mother, who's been dead for five years. Sandra looked very grown-up at that moment.

'It's six pounds fifty a week,' she said. 'Where are you going to get six pounds fifty a week?'

'We can pay it easy,' said Doris. 'That is, if your uncle'll only keep workin' steady . . .'

Her voice trailed away.

'And what does he say about it?'

'He doesn't know about it yet.'

'You'd better watch out for trouble when he comes in!' said Sandra grimly.

For a moment Doris looked apprehensive, and I wasn't surprised. Furniture wasn't the kind of thing that Walter would choose to spend his money on. But she soon recovered. She was quite excited, and not looking beyond the pleasure of the moment.

'The man from Widdowson's was right nice,' she said.

42

'A proper gentleman, not like old Nick Batten. He saw me lookin' in the shop winder, an' he come out specially to see if he could help me. Showed me all sorts of stuff, he did. Nothin' was too much trouble for him. An' he said they'd take it all back an' no questions asked if we decided not to keep it.'

Sandra looked relieved at this.

'It'll be on its way back before long!' she predicted.

But Doris didn't want that to happen.

'It's bin a proper tonic for me,' she said. 'I never had anything like it in all my life before. Eh, it was rough where I come from, down by the old Shambles, I can tell you. The Jungle was nothing to that. You kids don't know you're born. Coppers went round in pairs there, and the rent-collectors never went round at all, they wouldn't risk it. It was a filthy hole where I was brought up. Pulled down years ago, when the slum clearance first started. An' you know what?'

Doris was warming up now. It was one of the longest speeches I'd ever heard her make.

'You know what? It's like heaven to me, out here at Westwood. Heaven. An' it does something to me, havin' lovely stuff like this from Widdowson's. I don't want anything that reminds me of the Jungle. That's why I wish you hadn't been to Batten's. I wouldn't be surprised if your uncle wanted to keep what you've brought, an' send mine back to Widdowson's.'

'Well, I should hope he does,' said Sandra. 'What we've brought is paid for.'

For once, I felt Sandra's common sense was not quite enough. I had a glimmer of what was in Doris's mind, and I had a bit of sympathy with her. I could even, with a terrific effort, imagine Doris starting a new life. But there was no time to consider the situation, for just then we heard familiar tones from outside.

'Keep that flippin' cat away from me or I'll wring its neck!'

It was Walter addressing Jean as he came up the drive. Then we heard an exclamation as he saw the pile of furniture in front of the house. And finally Walter burst into the room – to stop in his tracks with surprise.

'An' what's – all – this?' he asked in a quiet, unpleasant voice.

Sandra and I are experts at judging Walter's moods. He was in a bad one today.

'You been gettin' things without tellin' me,' he said to Doris still quietly. 'Remember what I said I'd do to you for that?'

Doris got up and put the table between herself and Walter. She can judge his moods, too.

Walter turned to us and snarled: 'Flip off!' We retreated towards the kitchen. He continued addressing Doris in a quiet tone which we recognized as the most menacing of all.

'Where did all this come from?'

'Widdowson's.'

'They'll still be open. Go down there an' tell 'em to take it back.'

'I'm not goin' to.'

'We'll see about that.'

Walter moved round the table towards her. Doris dodged, keeping the table between them. Face to face with Walter she raised her voice defiantly.

'I'm sick of livin' like a pig! I wanted something nice for a change, an' I've got it, an' if you were any good you'd have got it yourself!'

'So. I'm no good, am I?' Walter was still speaking quietly.

'No, you great useless lout! Drinkin' an' backin' horses, that's all you're good for!'

Walter said nothing but made a sudden rapid movement. And Doris, dodging again, missed her step and came down with her full weight against the new sideboard. The front of it splintered.

Walter stood back as she got slowly to her feet. The steam went out of the row between them.

'We'll have to have it now!' said Doris. There was alarm in her voice. It struck me suddenly that she'd been playing out a fantasy. Deep down, she'd never really believed that the new furniture was here to stay.

'We'll see about that!' said Walter. He scowled. 'You stupid lump. We'll see about that!'

A shiny new car drew up at the garden gate, and a gentleman in a black overcoat got out of it. He was of medium height, plump and pink and very clean-looking, and he had spectacles with thick rims above the lenses and no rims underneath them.

'The manager from Widdowson's store!' said Sandra to me.

The gentleman beamed at us as he entered the drive.

'A beautiful evening!' he said in a juicy kind of voice. 'Don't you think it's a beautiful evening?'

'Yes, sir,' I said.

'Yes, of course it is. Beautiful. Now let me see, this is Mr Thompson's house, isn't it? You must be his children.'

'He's our uncle,' I said.

'Oh yes. Lucky man to have such a nice-looking niece and nephew. As a matter of fact, I've a boy and girl of my own at home, just your age, so I know what it is to have young people in the house. And I find it very pleasant, I may say, very pleasant. I won't hear a word against today's young people, and that's a fact.'

'I heard you tell a lady outside the shop that you had two tiny ones just like hers,' said Sandra coldly.

The gentleman appeared slightly shaken, but only for a moment.

'Yes, of course,' he said. 'I have two little ones. And two your age as well. Quite a family man. I love children, you know, really love them. It's always a joy to call at a house where there are children. There, let me offer you a toffee. You're not too big for toffees, are you? Of course not. Take some for the little ones as well. I always have time to talk to young people. It would be a sad world if we old fogies hadn't time for the young folk, wouldn't it? But duty calls, alas, duty calls. I must have a little talk with Mr Thompson. He's in, I suppose?'

'He's in all right,' said Sandra. She grimaced at me as the well-dressed gentleman, after half bowing to her, proceeded up the drive and rang the front-door bell.

'I wonder what they'll tell him,' she said.

'Walter'll tell him to take it all back,' I said. 'Come on, Sandra, let's go out. I'm tired of the whole business.'

'I want to know what's happening,' said Sandra stubbornly. And then: 'Look, we'll give them a minute or two to get settled in the sitting-room, then we can go and listen at the hatch.'

I stared at her.

'Eavesdropping!' I said. 'And you're the one who keeps telling us what we should and shouldn't do.'

Sandra took no notice. I could tell she was in one of her most determined moods, and it was no good arguing.

'Come along, Kevin,' she said. 'Quietly. Try not to be clumsy for once.'

We tiptoed in through the back door and placed ourselves at the service hatch between kitchen and sitting-room. It had only a thin wooden door, and you could hear quite well through it.

'Sit down, Mr Brindley,' Doris was saying in her most ladylike tones.

'Ah, yes,' said the juicy voice. 'This is our New World suite, isn't it? Let me congratulate you on your taste, Mrs Thompson. It's the best-designed suite we have. And very good value, too. You ladies know what you're about, I must say.'

'We don't want it!' said Walter emphatically.

We couldn't see Mr Brindley's face of course, but his tone of voice was quite unruffled.

'Come now, Mr Thompson,' he said. 'Your wife has made an excellent choice. We shall never be able to offer a suite like this at such a low price again.'

'We don't want it!' repeated Walter.

'He thinks we'd have a job to keep up the payments,' said Doris to Mr Brindley, apologetically.

'Well, let's see,' said Mr Brindley. 'Perhaps we could work out your commitments. Don't be embarrassed. I do it for very many people, I can assure you, and it's entirely private between us. Now, Mr Thompson, you would earn in a normal week . . . how much?'

'Never mind that,' growled Walter. 'I'm not havin' it, an' that's flat. You can arrange for the van to take it away, first thing on Monday morning.'

'But, Mr Thompson,' began Mr Brindley on a note of surprised protest, 'perhaps you don't understand. Your wife has agreed to buy this furniture. I have her signature on our order form.'

'She'd no business to,' said Walter.

'You said you'd take it back if we didn't like it, Mr Brindley,' said Doris timidly.

'A moment, madam,' said Mr Brindley. 'A moment. I said, as we say to all our customers, that we would take it back if it was not satisfactory.'

'Yes, well . . .'

'But in what respect is it not satisfactory, Mrs Thompson? A change of mind on your part doesn't make the furniture unsatisfactory, does it? Now we're reasonable people at Widdowson's, very reasonable people, and if we found you had taken on too great a commitment, we'd see if we could adjust it. But to suggest we should take it all back when your signature is on this document – no, Mrs Thompson, I don't think *that's* reasonable.'

'What about the cooling-off period?' Walter demanded, in the tone of one playing a trump card. 'We're allowed a cooling-off period under the law, aren't we? Well, we've cooled off. So you can just cancel the whole thing!'

There was silence. It seemed that for once Mr Brindley hadn't anything to say. Then Walter went on:

'The stuff's junk, anyroad! Just look at that sideboard. The front got bashed in with just a little shove.'

We heard a movement of chairs, and then Mr Brindley's voice again in a regretful tone.

'Dear, dear, Mr Thompson, that's a pity. It must have had rough treatment in the short time it's been here. But you can't expect us to take responsibility for that. I'm afraid you must go through with it now – it's a matter of deciding what payments you can meet.'

'I won't pay a penny,' said Walter, 'an' you can do what the hell you like. If you was to send me to prison I still wouldn't pay.'

'Send you to prison?' echoed Mr Brindley. 'I don't think there's any question of that . . .' And then his voice hardened.

'I knew I'd seen you before!' he said sharply. 'City magistrates' court, about a year ago. Stealing lead from a church roof, wasn't it?'

We couldn't see Walter's face, but he must have been startled because he didn't say a word. And Mr Brindley went on, without a trace of the gentlemanly tones he'd used before.

'Previous convictions, too. A bad lad, aren't you, in a small way?'

'I've done nothing in the last twelve months,' said Walter, and added defiantly:

'Anyroad, I'm not askin' to be a customer of yours. Now maybe you'll take the stuff away an' be done with it. An' if you want to know, we've got all the furniture upstairs we need – good solid second-hand stuff, much better than this.'

'Oh, you have, have you?' said Mr Brindley, still in the new sharp voice. There was silence for a minute, then he said: 'Well, I can't be sitting here all night. I'll be on my way.'

'An' what have we to do?' asked Doris nervously.

'I'll let you know later,' said Mr Brindley in a tone that shut her up completely. There was a shuffling of chairs, and we heard Doris's heels click as she went to fetch Mr Brindley's hat. And just as we were drawing away from the hatch we heard him speak again to Walter.

'Thompson,' he said (no 'Mister' this time), 'I want a word with you. Just walk down to the car with me, will you?'

Sandra and I slipped out of the house by the back door. We waited for a few minutes before going round to the front. And when we did we saw that Walter and Mr Brindley were still talking quietly together at the gate. As we approached, they separated. Mr Brindley saw us, but showed no sign of his previous friendliness, and climbed into his car without a word.

'Haven't you two got anything better to do than hang around?' said Walter automatically as he passed us and returned slowly to the house. He seemed – and this was unusual in Walter – to be deep in thought.

Sandra and I sat side by side on the low front wall.

'What did you make of it all?' I asked.

Sandra frowned.

'I don't know what to make of it,' she said. 'After that man found out about Walter stealing the lead his whole attitude changed, didn't it?'

'Well, that's not surprising,' I said.

'What do you think will happen, Kevin?'

'Oh, they won't want Walter as a customer now. I expect the furniture will go back to Widdowson's pretty quick. Then everybody'll be happy. Except Doris, maybe.'

Sandra had got down from the wall and wandered into the middle of the street. Now she called me over.

'There's Mr Brindley's car,' she said, 'parked outside the big house at the street corner, next to Westwood Road. You know whose house that is.'

'Alderman Widdowson's,' I said. 'Old Widdershins. I bet Mr Brindley's asking him what to do next.'

'There's something about all this that's worrying me,' said Sandra, 'but I don't know what it is.'

'It's just that you're a worrier,' I said. 'Forget it.' And thinking of old Widdershins I remembered something I'd read in a book.

'You know what Widdershins means, Sandra?' I said.

'I didn't know it meant anything.'

'It means going the wrong way round, right to left instead of left to right. You know, anti-clockwise. I think they used to draw a circle that way round in black magic, when they wanted to raise the devil.'

'Raising the devil!' said Sandra. 'People are always doing that, without needing any black magic.' She smiled faintly at her own little joke, but as she looked along the street towards that parked car outside Mr Widdowson's house she still didn't seem to be any too happy. 'We don't want anyone raising the devil here!' she said.

6

'Flip off out, all the lot o' you,' said Walter after breakfast next day. 'An' you needn't come back till teatime. A lovely day like this, you should be glad to be out. When I was a lad I was always out in the fresh air – unless I was helpin' my dad, of course. But kids aren't much help these days.'

Sandra and I looked at each other. It wasn't like Walter to suggest a day out for us.

'What about our dinner?' Sandra asked.

'Get yourselves some crisps,' said Walter. And still more surprisingly he pulled a couple of fifty-pence pieces out of his pocket and slung them to Sandra.

I felt a bit worried, remembering the previous day's events and wondering if for some reason Walter wanted us out of the way. I mentioned my suspicions to Sandra while we were washing up.

'I wouldn't be surprised,' she said. 'But we can't hang about all day in case anything happens, can we? And it *is* a lovely morning. Let's forget about everything and just enjoy ourselves.'

'What shall we do?'

'We'll get a 34 bus from the Parade and go right out to the terminus. That's Brightwell. It's a village up in the hills. We'll have a picnic.'

'We're expecting to do a lot for a pound, aren't we?' I said.

'Don't forget I've got two pounds fifty as well,' said Sandra.

'But listen. Mr Hedley said you'd to keep the five pounds that Mr Batten gave you back. Well, you didn't. You gave half to Doris for the rent money, and now you want to spend the rest on us. That's not keeping it.'

'I know what I'm doing,' said Sandra shortly. 'She needed the rent money, and we need a day out, and that's that.'

And it was no good arguing with her.

So by ten o'clock we were all four getting on board the 34 bus at Westwood Parade, all clean and tidy and looking forward to our picnic. Jean had wanted to bring Pussy, but we soon squashed that idea. And Harold had said something about wanting to play with his friends instead, but seeing that none of the Widdowson Crescent children ever seemed

51

all that keen to play with Harold we didn't take much notice and here he was with us.

We all got half fares on the bus. I sat nearest to the window and sort of shrank myself so as to look under fourteen. Even so, it was twenty pence each, and it would cost the same amount to come back. The bus ran through two or three miles of Westwood, and then the estate stopped suddenly at the county boundary and we were heading for the hills. It was a clear blue sunny Sunday, and Sandra and I were thrilled, because we'd really only been in the country once before, and then it was on a school outing and wasn't much fun. The ride lasted so long that the younger children began to get restless and bounce about a bit, but we kept them in order, even when at the end there was nobody but us aboard. And so we got off at the terminus at Brightwell at twenty to eleven, the bus being exactly on time.

Where the bus turned round, there was a tree in the middle of the road with a bench running right round it. And there was a shop that was open and that sold nearly everything. We bought four tenpenny ice-creams and sat on the bench while Sandra sorted out the money. Eighty pence for the bus journey back home, and one pound twenty we'd spent already – that made two pounds out of the three pounds fifty we'd had to start with. So we had one pound fifty to spend on the picnic. We bought four meat pies and four packets of crisps and a bottle of pop, and it just worked out exactly. And then we set off.

There was a lane with a stream flowing beside it, going down towards a lake a mile or two away, with hills on both sides. That seemed as good a way as any. Harold and Jean jumped backwards and forwards across the stream, and walked on stepping-stones and floated twigs and so on, and we didn't get along very fast, but they were enjoying themselves, so we didn't mind. After a while, seeing it didn't make much difference, I jumped the stream a few times and floated a few sticks myself, but Sandra just walked on the grass verge looking sedate and telling everybody off.

Then we saw, far up the hillside and overlooking the lake, a jutting-out crag. Harold claimed there was an eagle's nest up there, and we told him not to be daft, but he wouldn't be convinced and wanted to go and have a look.

'Well, it would be a good spot for the picnic,' said Sandra.

So we headed up the hillside, and it was a good deal further to the crag than it seemed. But we got there in the end, and it was a lovely place, a little platform of grey stone. You could climb all round it, and it was quite safe, the drop being never more than a few feet to the hillside, even though you seemed to be right up above the world.

Harold and Jean were still full of energy, and went clambering over the stone and rolling down the slope and so on. But Sandra and I just lay flat on the top of the crag and looked at the view and talked to each other a bit, but not about our problems because we'd decided not to.

I mentioned that it was only a few days now before Dick and his parents moved out to Westwood, and Sandra looked a bit dreamy, she being very fond of the Hedleys. And I began to have a strange feeling as I lay there on top of the crag looking down at the lake, which had yachts on it. It was getting quite warm now, but pleasant because there was just a tiny bit of breeze. And I started feeling sad, but in quite a nice way, which was puzzling. I thought perhaps I was happy, but I wasn't sure. For quite a while I didn't say anything to Sandra, and I wondered if she was dozing off.

Then I heard voices, not the children's. It sounded like a man and a woman approaching. But actually it was a boy and girl, not much older than ourselves, who clambered on to the rock and sat down at the other edge, a few feet away from us.

I wouldn't have recognized them, but Sandra sat up straight and whispered in my ear : 'David and Anne Widdowson.'

The girl smiled at us and said, 'Hello!' quite pleasantly,

53

and her brother said, 'Hello!' too, and then they just chatted to each other in ordinary tones, neither louder nor softer than usual, as if there was nobody there.

I felt awkward, because although they were wearing old clothes they were still in a subtle way much better dressed than we were, and their way of speaking was different. And the boy's voice had broken completely and was low and pleasant like a man's, whereas mine at this time was still a bit doubtful and sometimes went into a squeak. I felt inclined to clear off and leave the crag to them, but when I whispered the suggestion to Sandra she whispered back that she didn't see why we should, and on reflection neither did I.

So for quite a while the Widdowsons talked, and Sandra and I just whispered to each other now and again. Soon I became interested in them, and was glad we hadn't moved. They were a good deal alike, both having dark curly hair and brown skins and very white teeth. I thought they were both very good-looking. In fact I couldn't stop casting glances at Anne. She had taken off her windcheater and was wearing a bright yellow jumper, and after a minute or two she lay back with her head on her clasped hands and her hair let out.

Sandra dug me in the ribs and told me not to stare, but I knew nobody had noticed except her. Sandra notices everything.

Then there was a scrabbling, and Harold and Jean climbed up on to the crag, wanting to know if it was dinnertime. It was only just after twelve, but Sandra and I felt quite hungry too, so we unpacked the picnic, and we each had a meat pie and a packet of crisps and a swig of orangeade. It had looked a good picnic when we bought it, but among four of us it didn't seem to go very far.

As we finished, David and Anne Widdowson began unpacking *their* picnic. It wasn't a bit like ours, in fact it was rather too fancy for my liking (not that I'd have refused it). They had a crusty foreign loaf, and butter in a little dish, and

54

half a chicken, and some salad in a polythene bag, and hard-boiled eggs and biscuits and cheese and a bottle of milk. Harold and Jean were fascinated and crept towards them, eyeing all this, until Sandra called them back. But David said: 'They aren't annoying us at all,' so then Harold and Jean went and sat beside them, as bold as brass, and made remarks about the things they were eating, and were given bits of this and that to taste.

The Widdowsons smiled across at us, being amused by the children's behaviour, but Sandra was furious.

'You'd think we were beggars!' she said in a fierce whisper.

But for once I managed to restrain her, pointing out that a bit of good food wouldn't do the young ones any harm, and this was a point that counted with Sandra even more than pride. So she sat rather unhappily with her back to all the goings-on, pretending it was nothing to do with her.

After a while Anne Widdowson caught my eye and said:

'I don't think we'll ever finish all this. Could you possibly help us?'

I felt Sandra stiffen.

'We're all right,' she said, 'thank you.'

'I didn't really want the nuisance of taking it home,' Anne said. 'So it would be a favour –'

'We're all right, thank you!' repeated Sandra in a snub-bing kind of voice. Anne raised her eyebrows. I thought it would be politer to accept the offer. Besides, I was still quite hungry. Also I am not as proud as Sandra.

'I'll have some,' I said, and moved over. So then Sandra had to come too, as she couldn't have sat on her own in the corner, and we all helped to finish off the picnic, down to the last crumb. But Sandra was still sulky and wouldn't say much except 'Yes' and 'No', thus giving a rather poor impression of herself, which is quite wrong, Sandra being by far the best person of all of us.

When we had finished, Anne gathered up the scraps and

old papers and put them in her haversack. Jean was romping all over David, and demanding to be thrown up in the air and caught and so on, so he went off and played with both children on the hillside. And I talked to Anne and was not shy at all. She was interested to hear about the special scholarship that Harold could sit for, and said he seemed very bright. This pleased Sandra, who began to come round a bit. Then Sandra told Anne about the essay prize I'd won last year. But what interested her most of all was when Sandra mentioned that I could tell stories. Then Anne looked at me with so much respect I felt embarrassed.

'I don't know anybody who can do things like that,' she said. 'All our friends can play games and ride and so on, but they'd never think of telling stories, even if they could. And they can't.'

'Well, I just do it sometimes to amuse the young ones,' I said.

'You don't have to apologize,' said Anne, and she smiled at me, showing those very white teeth. 'I mean, anybody can play games if they've been taught. Well, nearly anybody. But if you can't tell stories, you can't. Look at David there. He hasn't even the imagination to tell a good lie.'

I looked at David. He was boxing Harold, and Harold was having a high old time, thinking he was winning. He didn't realize that David was only playing with him. We all grinned.

'He's getting a car for his seventeenth birthday next week,' Anne said, and pulled a slight face. 'Then he won't have any time for walking with me.'

Sandra and I exchanged looks. We couldn't really imagine a kind of life where you got a car for your birthday, just like that. And obviously Anne took it as a matter of course. She wasn't even terribly pleased about it. She went on talking to me for quite a while, mostly about books. It was a disappointment when she suddenly sprang to her feet, dusted herself down, and called to David that it was time they were getting along. And David shook off the two younger children, though he was grinning all the time, and they just said a casual good-bye to us and went on their way.

'Don't look so glum,' said Sandra a minute later.

'I'm not looking glum.'

'Yes, you are. Well, you needn't think any more about those Widdowsons. They just happened to run into us, but it doesn't mean anything to them – why should it?'

'She offered to lend me a book,' I said.

'She'll forget,' said Sandra, and added grimly: 'The next dealings we'll probably have with that family will be their father putting the bailiffs in.'

'Now then, you know what you said,' I reminded her. 'We're not going to talk about all that.'

And we both cheered up. In fact we had a lovely day. We went down to the lake and the younger ones paddled and Jean collected an armful of wild flowers, though they soon started to wilt. We caught the half past six bus back to Westwood and got off at the Parade and walked up to our own street. It was still fine and sunny. We'd hardly noticed how the days were getting longer. Everybody seemed to be in their gardens. Nobody had got a lawn made yet except at No. 11, where a smooth patch of green grass and two or three vivid flower-beds had appeared by magic. All the men were digging, when they weren't gossiping, and the women were in summer frocks, and there were lots of young children dashing about on scooters and tri-cycles and pushing dolls' prams. It was a cheerful, busy scene.

And when we got to No. 17 we had a surprise which to Sandra at least was a very pleasant one. All the new furniture had gone, and Walter wasn't there, and Doris was polishing away at the stuff we'd brought from Batten's, and it didn't look at all bad.

Sandra hummed a little tune as she got us something to

57

eat. I know Sandra as well as she knows me, and I could tell she was unusually happy. The house was furnished, with furniture that was paid for. Doris was showing signs of pulling herself together, and although it might not last, it was promising. Walter's absence certainly would not last, but – well, we had lived with Walter a long time and had learned to put up with him, and even Walter was all right, sometimes. Soon Dick Hedley and his parents would have moved to Westwood and would be living just round the corner from us. That would be a great comfort to Sandra. And we had a carpet in the sitting-room.

We didn't see Walter that evening, but we heard him later on, when it was obvious that he had come back from the Dragon. On Monday morning we couldn't get him out of bed, and that was not too surprising. At Monday teatime we came home from school to find him in a good mood. He had backed a winner at six to one, and was very pleased with himself. Sandra was given money to buy fish fingers for tea as a special treat. And we were just sitting down to it when there was a timid knock at the back door. It was Mrs Robbins from No. 19, where Harold had been playing occasionally in the past week or two.

Walter was delighted to see her. He steered her into an armchair and hovered around her. But his smile faded as it became clear that this wasn't just a social call.

Mrs Robbins was nervous but determined.

'It's about your Harold,' she began.

Walter was familiar with this way of opening an interview.

'What's he done?' he demanded.

'Well, it's – I'm afraid it's money.'

'What do you mean, Mrs Robbins?'

'I mean – well, I kept missing money off the sideboard, and it was always when he'd just been in.'

'Our Harold never took it,' said Walter firmly.

58

'Well, he must have done,' said Mrs Robbins, still timid but meaning to see it through. 'Last time was on Sat'day. Harold came in to see if our Leslie was playin', and I told him Leslie had gone down to his auntie's, and my back was only turned a minute. And when Harold had gone, a pound note had gone as well.'

We all looked at Harold. And from his face there was no doubt that he was guilty. He went first red, then white, and stayed white, with his eyes wide open, staring.

'Have you taken money from Mrs Robbins?' asked Sandra in a quiet voice.

Harold just nodded.

'Well, you little nit!' said Walter – in disgust with Harold for being found out, I thought, rather than for stealing.

'I knew it must be him before that,' Mrs Robbins said in an apologetic tone. 'He kept having sweets and giving them to the other kiddies, and I was sure he couldn't be getting all that much pocket-money.'

This seemed to rankle with Walter.

'What d'you mean, he couldn't be gettin' all that much pocket-money? I can afford to give my lad pocket-money if I want.'

Mrs Robbins was silent, but Walter, with a grand gesture, pulled a wad of notes from his trousers pocket.

'You needn't think we're short of a few pounds here, Mrs Robbins,' he said.

Everyone in the room stared at the wad of money. We had never seen anything like it before. Walter seldom had money in his pocket for long.

'Now, how much do you reckon he's had of yours, Mrs Robbins?' Walter went on. 'Just you tell me an' I'll give it back to you.'

'Oh, it doesn't matter,' Mrs Robbins said uneasily. 'It's not the money, it's just that we thought you ought to know what was going on.'

'Here, take a fiver. Does that cover it?'

Mrs Robbins was embarrassed, and wouldn't take the note from Walter's hand. In some odd way he seemed to have worked himself into a position of moral superiority.

'If you leave money lying about, you know, kids'll take it,' said Walter in a man-of-the-world tone. 'You want to look after it in future.'

'Well, I mean, you don't expect it to disappear in your own home,' said Mrs Robbins in half-hearted protest.

'You can't be too careful,' said Walter. He was jaunty now. 'There, just you take this, Mrs Robbins. Don't think no more about it. I'll handle the whole matter.'

He showed her out, putting his arm nearly round her shoulders to open the door. Mrs Robbins, who had been uneasy all the time, seemed relieved to get away.

'Where *did* you get all that money?' asked Doris as the door closed.

'Mind yer own flippin' business.'

'You can't have won all that on a horse.'

'I never said I did.'

'Well, then, where'd it come from?'

Walter took no notice.

'Here, Harold,' he said. 'Don't get caught doin' that again or I'll tan your backside. Now, you want some money, eh? Take this.'

He thrust a five-pound note into Harold's hand.

Walter has always been more indulgent to Harold than to the rest of us. I suppose it is because Harold is his son, and in his own way Walter is fond of him.

But this was too much. Harold would have cleared off, thanking his lucky stars, but Sandra and I collared him as he went down the drive. We took him into a corner of the building site.

'What did you do it for, Harold?' asked Sandra quietly.

Harold hung his head and said nothing.

'You know you shouldn't take what isn't yours?'

Harold nodded.

'Well, it stands to reason,' I said, butting in. 'You've got to be able to trust people. If nobody could put anything down without somebody else pinching it, life'd be impossible . . .'

Sandra shushed me. She is not given to theorizing.

'Harold, what you did was wrong,' she said. 'It was ever so wrong.'

Harold nodded again. He couldn't bring himself to speak.

'If you wanted money so much, why didn't you tell me?' Sandra went on.

Harold's eyes filled with tears.

'You never have any,' he said.

This was true, of course. It was unusual for any of us to have money.

'What did you buy with it?' Sandra asked in a softer tone.

Harold was slowly breaking down into sobs.

'I b-b-bought s-s-sweets,' he said.

'And ate them all yourself, you little pig?' I said in disgust.

Sandra shushed me again.

'You didn't eat them all yourself, did you, Harold?'

Harold shook his head.

'You gave them to the other children?'

Harold nodded.

Sandra didn't ask anything more. She knew – and at last I knew – what Harold had done it for. Poor kid, he wanted to make the others like him, and he thought he could do it by giving them sweets.

I'd have given him a talk explaining that this idea never worked anyway, but poor Harold was past being lectured to. He burst into great big sobs. Sandra took him into her arms.

He cried for a long time. I was glad nobody came.

'Don't do it again, Harold,' Sandra kept whispering. 'Never do it again.' And of course Harold promised he wouldn't. I knew he meant it. He was all right at heart. I felt rather bad, because I was the eldest and I ought to have been thinking more about Harold. I'd been so occupied with other problems that I hadn't realized he might have problems too.

'What shall we do about that five pounds?' I asked, meaning the money that Walter had thrust upon Harold.

Harold silently put the note into Sandra's hand.

'I'll keep it, the way I was supposed to keep the other one,' Sandra said. 'For emergencies. There's always liable to be emergencies.'

I sighed.

'You don't need to tell me that!' I said.

7

Walter didn't go to work next day, or for the rest of the week. We only saw him at teatimes, but we heard plenty from Doris. He still hadn't told her where he got the money, but he was lying in bed every morning and hanging round the betting-shop on the Parade each afternoon. And every evening he went round to the Dragon. What annoyed Doris was that he went without her.

'Says I'm gettin' old,' she complained. 'Says I'm no fun to have around. I keep tellin' him, he's as old as me, but he says that's different.' She consoled herself with polishing the furniture and grumbling.

We didn't think Walter could be winning much on the horses, because his good temper didn't last, and when we saw him at teatimes he was always scowling. On Saturday morning we were all rather late up, and Walter came down while Sandra was still making the breakfast. He looked white and had a big bruise on his forehead.

'Where's that flamin' cat?' he demanded. 'I fell over it when I came in last night. I'm takin' it to the animals' dispensary, to have it put down.'

Jean jumped up.

'He's my cat!' she cried.

'He won't be anybody's cat after this mornin'.'

'You mustn't touch him!'

'Oh, mustn't I?' said Walter grimly. 'I'll wring his flippin' neck in front of your flippin' eyes if you're not careful.'

Jean flew at him with her fists. Walter stood it for a moment, then gave her a clout that knocked her back a few feet.

Sandra intervened by calling everybody for breakfast. Walter took his bread-and-dripping in one hand and his mug of tea in the other, and wandered over to the glass to inspect his bruise. Jean watched him sullenly.

'You needn't think I don't mean it,' he told her. 'I've got something to remind me, I have. That brute's had its chips.'

Then Doris padded in with the post. We don't get much mail as a rule, but this particular Saturday there were two letters and a card. And Doris was staring at the card.

'What's this about, Walter Thompson?' she demanded.

'What's what about?'

'Take a look at it.'

Doris handed the card to Sandra, who handed it to me to give to Walter. So Sandra and I were both able to see what it said. It was a brief printed message:

WIDDOWSONS (COBCHESTER) LTD
16, The Parade, Higher Westwood
Quality Furnishers

Kindly note that the instalment on your
esteemed purchase is overdue and should
be paid at the above branch without delay.

'I thought you sent that furniture back to Widdowson's,' said Doris. 'How come they're askin' for money?'

'Must be a mistake,' muttered Walter uneasily.

We have often thought Doris dim-witted, but this time she was quick enough on the uptake.

'Mistake, nothin'!' she said. 'You flogged it, didn't you? That's where all that money came from.'

Walter didn't say anything, but looked as guilty as Harold had looked a few days earlier.

'You flippin' nit!' said Doris. 'They can get you for that. They got my cousin Albert. Flogged his motor-bike when it was still on H.P. It's an offence, that is.'

'They won't do anything if you keep on payin',' said Walter defensively.

'Keep on payin'? What you goin' to keep on payin' with? Anyway, where's the cash you got? Has it all gone?'

'I had a bit o' bad luck,' said Walter.

'You've lost the lot?'

Walter made a gesture of turning his pockets out.

'How much was it?'

'Eighty quid.'

'I'd like to set eyes on the chap who gave it you. I wondered why it was a lorry what come for that furniture last Sunday instead of a van with Widdowson's written all over it. I might have guessed. Come on, who did you flog it to?'

'It's nothing to do with you,' said Walter sullenly.

'Nothing to do with me, is it?' said Doris, and added with heavy sarcasm: 'Bit o' quick work for once in your life. We only got the stuff on Sat'day afternoon, an' by Sunday tea-time you'd sold it. You can move fast when you feel like it, can't you, Walter Thompson?'

Sandra and I had listened in silence to this dialogue. I was puzzled, and was wondering how the visit of Widdowson's manager, Mr Brindley, fitted into the story. Now Sandra spoke up with quiet passion.

'So!' she said in the tone that always reminds me of our mother. 'You got eighty pounds cash, and you've lost it all on the horses, and now you've to go on paying six pounds fifty a week for the next two years. That's a fine bargain!'

Even Walter winced at the scorn in her voice. He fumbled nervously with one of the two envelopes that were still unopened.

'Well, you'll have to get up in the mornings an' go to work now,' commented Doris, 'or heaven help the lot of us!'

But Walter had turned whiter than ever.

'Some hope!' he said. He sat down heavily. 'This letter's from my boss. Vincent's have sent me my cards. Habitual non-attendance. They say I've had enough warnings. They've given me the flippin' sack!'

Doris stared at him. We had often seen her depressed or complaining, but it was rarely that she showed anything as positive as anger. Now I could feel her coming to the boil.

'You – great – useless – lout!' she said slowly. And then, gathering speed:

'Here we are with a chance to start afresh an' forget all that's gone. An' look what you do. Muck it up as usual, that's what! I'm sick to death of you, Walter Thompson. You're as low as a louse!'

Walter was going to hit her, but Sandra managed to get in the way, and he wouldn't dare to hit Sandra. To make a diversion Sandra said:

'You haven't opened that other letter.'

Walter opened the letter that was still in his hand.

'It's from your Uncle Bob, over in Yorkshire,' he said. And then, a moment later:

'He's sent us twenty quid!'

Uncle Bob is Walter's brother. There were three brothers, the third being my father who is dead. Uncle Bob has always helped us when he can, but he doesn't earn high wages and he has a crippled wife, so there is a limit to what he can do.

There was a letter with the money:

Dear Walter,

Hope you are settling down in new house. I expect it will all be very strange and many expenses as I know having moved to corporation house myself two years ago and it was all pay pay pay, hope the enclosed will be of assistance, buy Sandra a new dress if not needed for anything else, Flora is a bit better now winter is over but can't expect much change, well Walter I must close for now and go shopping, hope all are well,

Your Brother,
Bob

Walter beamed all over his face.

'Good old Bob!' he said. 'I might have known he'd turn up trumps!'

'Well, it's come at the right time,' said Doris. 'You can give me some of it to start with, or I don't know what we'll have to eat this week-end. An' there's the rent to pay on Monday.'

'Haven't got no change,' said Walter cheerfully.

'Give it me. I'll get it changed,' Doris offered.

'Oh no you don't. He sent it to me, not you.'

'It was to help us all.'

'I'll give you all you need by tonight,' said Walter, 'an' more as well.'

'You mean you'll lose it on another flippin' horse,' predicted Doris.

'What are you going to do about Widdowsons?' asked Sandra quietly.

But now that Walter had money in his pocket he wasn't standing for any questions.

'You shut up,' he told Sandra. 'Gettin' too big for your boots, that's what you are. When I was your age I wasn't always tellin' my elders an' betters what to do. You'll get a tannin', big as you are, if you don't watch out.'

Walter went off whistling. Doris sank into a chair, and produced (as she always could in times of stress) a crumpled cigarette from somewhere in her overall.

'Well, he's got us into this mess, he'll 'ave to get us out of it,' she said. 'I'm past botherin', an' that's a fact.'

Sandra's eyes met mine. I wondered if she had something to suggest. But before she could say anything a round, pretty face appeared in the doorway.

'I wondered if your Harold could come out for the day with us,' said Mrs Robbins. 'He's been playin' with Leslie all week as good as gold, and they don't want to be parted.'

'Oh, aye, I suppose so,' said Doris indifferently.

'By the way,' Mrs Robbins went on, 'did you know your little lass had gone off on the bus, all on her own?'

Sandra and I were startled. Jean had slipped out after bolting a few mouthfuls of breakfast, but we hadn't thought anything of it. Doris was still unmoved.

'I just saw her gettin' on the city bus at the corner,' continued Mrs Robbins. 'She had that cat draped round her neck, an' she was carryin' a big brown-paper parcel. She's a bit small to be goin' into Cobchester on her own, isn't she? I wondered if you knew about it.'

'You know more than I do, as usual,' said Doris from her chair.

'Oh, I didn't mean to poke my nose in!' said Mrs Robbins hastily. 'I was just worried a bit about the little girl, you know.'

'I wish *I* had nothin' to worry about but other folks' business,' said Doris.

Mrs Robbins shrugged her shoulders helplessly and withdrew without another word. When she had gone, Sandra turned to me.

'I bet Jean's gone off with Pussy,' she said, 'to save him from being put away. Oh, Kevin, let's – '

'Yes,' I said. I knew what she was going to say. 'Let's go and see Dick!'

The Hedleys had moved to their new house, which was not far from ours, a couple of days earlier. Generally Sandra is too proud to go to other people about our troubles. She'd rather wrestle with them on her own. But the Hedleys are an exception. Especially Dick. It seems to come naturally to Sandra to share her burdens with Dick.

The Hedleys' house was No. 24 Forest Walk. It was the next street to Widdowson Crescent, and the 'forest' was the spinney that lay between them. There were only about twenty trees – not much of a forest, you might say, but I suppose it gets hard to think of street names for a big place like Westwood Estate.

When we got to No. 24 it took us quite a while to make ourselves heard above the sounds of hammering and vacuum-cleaning that were going on inside. Eventually Mrs Hedley came to the door. She was wearing a man's boiler-suit, and a beret that covered every scrap of hair, and she had the nozzle of the vacuum-cleaner in her hand. She looked like a small, elderly soldier going into battle.

'Eh, there's that much to do, I don't think I'll get through it this side of Christmas,' she said. 'Nay, you're not interruptin' me. It's time I gave myself a rest. That hammerin' you can hear, that's our Dick puttin' up a shelf in the bathroom. Go an' fetch him, Sandra love, he'll never hear us with all that row he's makin'.'

Mrs Hedley smiled her rare, thin-lipped smile as Sandra disappeared towards the stairs. Dick's mother is a tough, shrewd little woman, and has a sharp tongue when roused, but she is always kind to us.

'I love your Sandra like a daughter, I do that,' she'd told me once. 'And I'll have her for a daughter some day, if our Dick has any sense. You mark my words.' But this was something I'd never dared to mention to Sandra.

The hammering stopped, and after a minute or two Dick came running downstairs – 'like a herd of elephants,' commented Mrs Hedley.

68

'I've got to go out, Mum,' Dick announced. 'Sorry, can't help it. Very urgent. I'll finish that job later.'

'Go on, off you go,' said Mrs Hedley. 'I can get on all the better for a bit of peace. I'm not sorry your dad's at work to-day, I can tell you. Lads an' men alike, you only get in the way.'

She looked up into his face. At sixteen Dick is a head taller than his mother. But she always makes it clear who's in charge.

'You wash your face before you go out!' she told him sharply.

Dick ran his fingers through his red hair and splashed water into his face from the kitchen sink, and got out of the house quickly, before he could be inspected. Sandra and I said hasty farewells to Mrs Hedley and followed. As we went down the path we heard the roar of the vacuum-cleaner. Mrs Hedley was in action once more.

'Well now,' said Dick, in the confident tone that always convinced us he knew just what to do, 'Jean will have gone back to the Jungle, there's no doubt about that. And so much of the Jungle's been pulled down that I reckon we'll find her quite easily; there's nowhere much to hide. And while we're there we can talk to Tony Boyd. He might be able to help us with the other problems.'

'Talk to Tony?' I said. 'Don't be daft, Dick. You know he left St Jude's eighteen months ago.'

Tony was the Reverend Anthony Boyd. He had formerly been curate of St Jude's, the parish next to the Jungle, and he and his fiancée Sheila had been a great help to us at the time of our troubles two years previously. But he had been transferred to another parish, somewhere in the Midlands. I didn't see how Dick could have forgotten this.

'Aha!' said Dick triumphantly. 'I know something you don't. I only heard it the other day. Tony's come back to St Jude's. The old vicar retired, and Tony's the vicar now. They couldn't get him back quick enough!'

Suddenly I felt a hundred per cent more cheerful. Tony Boyd is all right, in spite of wearing a dog-collar. With him and Sheila and Dick to help us, we'd get by.

'Come on, then!' said Dick. 'No time to waste. Next bus into town. Quick march to the bus stop.'

'Don't be bossy, Dick!' I said.

'Do as you're told, Kevin!' said Sandra.

8

'It's good to see you!' said the Reverend Anthony Boyd. He stood on the hearthrug at St Jude's Vicarage and beamed at each of us in turn through his spectacles. He had filled out a bit in the last two years, and was now a big man, rather than the tall thin one he'd been before. He still looked just what he was: cheerful and friendly, and at the same time decidedly tough.

'You're all looking well,' he went on. 'Quite a change from the old days. I expect it's that Westwood air. I must call Sheila.' And in a moment Mrs Boyd, who had formerly been Miss Woodrow and had taken me for English at the old Camellia Hill Modern School, was greeting us. She was going to have a baby and was getting quite fat with it, but she looked very pretty and happy.

'We're looking for Jean,' Dick explained. And we told Tony and Sheila what had happened.

Tony pulled a face.

'And you've no idea where she might be, except that you think she'd probably come back to the Jungle?'

'She'd be looking for a place where she could go with

Pussy,' I said. 'It's daft, but she's only eight years old, and she does love that cat. We might find her in a derelict house, like we did a few weeks ago, the day we left here.'

'In that case,' said Tony, 'I think she'll have had enough by the time it's dark, or probably before. And if she can make her way here she can probably make her way home.'

'Yes, but poor little soul,' said Sheila, 'she'd be scared stiff long before night-time.'

Tony nodded. 'That's true,' he said. 'We'd better find her. But where . . .?'

And then, as light dawned in Sheila's face, we all thought of the answer at once.

'Gumble's Yard!' she said. 'I remember so well when you were at Gumble's Yard. Jean said she wanted to live there for ever and ever. So do you think . . .?'

And we all did think. Two years ago, when Sandra and Harold and Jean and I had tried to fend for ourselves in an old attic in Gumble's Yard, the rest of us had been very unhappy, but Jean had had a lovely time. She'd been too young to realize what was going on.

'I bet she's in Gumble's Yard now!' said Sandra with conviction. 'Setting up house with Pussy!'

'Well, let's go and see!' said Tony.

As Vicar, Tony was a little more prosperous than he'd been when he was a curate. Outside St Jude's Vicarage stood a very small, rather old car. Dick and Sandra and I squeezed into the back, Tony and Sheila into the front, and it made a pretty full load.

We crossed Camellia Hill and drove down Hibiscus Street. There was hardly a house to be seen by now, though the George Inn was still standing. Tony had to be careful because bricks and all kinds of junk lay scattered in the roadway. Along Canal Street most of the old warehouses had been pulled down some months before. But at the far end, near the railway viaduct, the disused buildings of

71

Gumble's Yard were still there. Tony stopped the car at the point, a few yards from the canal bank, where a door at second-floor level opened straight into space. Behind it lay the attic that we had once called our 'homestead'.

The door was closed. Dick threw two or three pebbles against it, but there was no response. Of the two small windows, one was broken, the other crusted with dirt. The fall-pipe, up which we had once climbed to get to that doorway, was missing now. To me the place didn't seem as if it could possibly be occupied, and I felt with dismay that we were no nearer to tracing Jean. But Dick was more optimistic.

'If she's here, she must have got in from inside the building,' he said. And he led the way to the dark corner inside the end cottage where there was a trapdoor to the attic.

A system of footholds made the trapdoor accessible. Dick climbed up and banged hard on the underside. Still there was no response. Dick pushed at the trap, but it didn't move. He came back to ground level and we all looked at each other ruefully, no longer really thinking that Jean could be there.

Then, unmistakably, we heard the mew of a cat.

Silently and at once, Dick shinned up to the trapdoor again and pushed it quickly. This time it gave way. A moment later he was through.

'There you are, Jeannie!' we heard him cry. And then there was the sound of loud sobbing from Jean.

Tony and I followed Dick up through the trapdoor. Sheila stayed below, saying she was too fat for getting through trapdoors just now, and at first Sandra stayed with her. But Jean refused to talk to any of us, and kicked and screamed if we tried to touch her, so we had to call to Sandra to come up. On seeing Sandra, Jean at first turned her head to the wall and went on sobbing in a forced way. But after a minute or so she ran to Sandra, as she and Harold had done ever since they were tiny, to be held in her arms.

'I'm not going back there!' was the first thing she said as the sobs died down.

'But why not, love?' said Sandra. 'It's nice at Westwood and we're all together. You couldn't stay here, you know you couldn't.'

'I could. I shall stay here with Pussy. My dad said he'd have Pussy put down, and I won't let him.'

Pussy had shrunk into a corner. I looked at him. Even in the poor light you could see what a scarred and ugly beast he was. Sandra sighed.

'We'll do what we can to keep him,' she said. 'But honestly – '

'He's a *nice* cat!' said Jean.

Pussy arched and spat as Tony stretched out a hand towards him.

'It's only because of the way he's been treated,' said Jean. 'Look, he's all right with me.' And, indeed, when Jean approached him, Pussy purred and rubbed round her ankles.

But Jean was beginning to give way. Even at eight years old she knew really that she couldn't stay in Gumble's Yard. She'd had the satisfaction of walking out, and of having attracted everybody's attention. She was ready to settle – after a show of resistance – for Sandra's promise to try to get Walter to keep Pussy. In a minute or two she was clinging round Sandra's neck.

'You'll look after me, won't you, Sandra?' she said. 'Me and Pussy. And Harold. You'll look after us, won't you, 'cause you always do.'

'I'll look after you,' Sandra assured her.

But as we returned to the tiny car, into which we now had to pack another person and an animal, I heard Sandra sigh, and I thought, not for the first time, that we all expected an awful lot from her.

*

Jean sat in a rocking-chair in a corner of the Vicarage sitting-room. She was happy now. Pussy lay on her lap, purring. He had an enormous purr, that cat, like a motor-bike revving up, or nearly.

Dick and Sandra and I now had to explain the trouble we were in because of the furniture that had to be paid for although we hadn't got it any more, and because of Walter's lost job. Dick, as usual, did most of the talking. Now and then I corrected him or added a few words, but Sandra just sat looking glum. She hated having to ask for help, even from people we knew as well as Tony and Sheila.

When Dick mentioned Alderman Widdowson, Tony looked thoughtful.

'I've met Mr Widdowson two or three times,' he said. 'A strange man, and I don't quite know what to make of him. Very efficient in the city council, but I sometimes wonder what he's in it *for*. He doesn't strike me as public-spirited, and I'm sure he's not in public life for the glory of it . . .'

'He sells rotten furniture,' said Sandra.

'You can say that again!' said Dick. 'My dad says all Widdowson's stuff is rubbish. And he says you couldn't even *give* it to old Nick Batten second-hand – he wouldn't have it in the shop.'

'I wouldn't know about that,' said Tony. 'I've never heard anything against Mr Widdowson myself. He's said to be a reasonable man. He could get you off the hook if he felt like it. I think I'd better talk to him.'

'Even if we got the debt sorted out,' I said, 'we'd still be in trouble unless my uncle could get a job fairly soon.'

'I know,' said Tony. He frowned. 'And that's not too easy. I could probably get him a job, but – '

'But would he keep it?' I asked.

'And would it be fair to ask anybody to employ him?' said Sandra, guessing more accurately what was in Tony's mind.

Tony smiled slightly.

'Of course, I could give your uncle a talking-to,' he said. 'That seemed to have some effect last time.'

'It might last for a week,' said Sandra dryly.

'Oh well, let's deal with Widdowson first, and see what happens,' said Tony. 'I wonder if he'll be at home on a Saturday afternoon. Pass me that telephone book, will you, Dick?'

'I ought really to have made you come to my surgery,' said Alderman Widdowson. 'I call it my surgery, you know, when I'm at home to hear about people's troubles in my ward. But I gather this concerns me as a businessman rather than as an alderman.'

We were in the big Widdowson house, at the corner of our own street and Westwood Road. Alderman Widdowson had received us in his study, and he now smiled at Tony: a faint, chilly smile.

He was a man of about fifty, cool and self-assured, with a pale face and very smooth dark hair, perfectly groomed.

Tony told the story of our furniture once more. Mr Widdowson listened in silence, tut-tutting (though not sounding particularly surprised or shocked) when Tony told him that it had all been sold for cash although it was on hire-purchase. Tony finished by painting a glowing picture of how Sandra and I had struggled to hold the family together over the years. Sandra bit her lip and looked daggers at Tony, and even I was a bit embarrassed. Mr Widdowson listened with polite interest and commented, in a slightly dry tone, 'Highly creditable.' Then he was silent for a minute.

'I'd like to help you, Mr Boyd,' he said eventually, 'or, rather, I'd like to help your young protégés. You'll realize that it isn't easy, though. Quite apart from owing us money, this man Thompson has committed an offence.'

'I realize that,' said Tony.

'He has a rather poor record, too, I gather,' said Mr

75

Widdowson. 'I don't suppose the courts would be very sympathetic towards him. On the other hand, I never like to get a man into trouble. I think it might be best, Mr Boyd, if we forget what you've just told me about Thompson's illegal disposal of our goods and treat this simply as a case of a man who can't keep up his payments. Now, what can we do to put him in a position to pay off his account?'

Once again he paused for a moment. Then:

'I could use an extra man at my warehouse. I wonder if Thompson would fill the bill? It's just ordinary manual work, loading and unloading, but I don't suppose he's qualified for anything better.'

Tony's eyes shone.

'That would be splendid,' he said.

'It's only a thought,' said Mr Widdowson, in a slightly snubbing tone. 'You'll agree that it's rather a risk, taking on a man like that.'

'Quite true,' said Tony ruefully.

'Do you feel you could guarantee his good conduct?'

'Frankly, no,' said Tony. 'I'd do what I could, that's all.'

I began to think the idea of a job at Widdowson's for Walter wasn't going to work out. Mr Widdowson hadn't spoken with any warmth all through the interview, and he certainly didn't seem like the kind of man who would give people jobs out of charity. I was surprised when he said:

'I think I might risk it, all the same. Send Thompson to see me next week. I shall be at the warehouse myself on Wednesday afternoon. Tell him to be there at four o'clock prompt. I'm not promising anything, but if he seems at all possible as an employee I might give him a chance.'

'He held down his last job for over a year,' said Tony, 'so he can work steadily if he feels like it. I think it was partly the distance he had to travel to work that caused him to backslide.'

'Well, he wouldn't have far to go if he worked for me,' said

Mr Widdowson. 'The warehouse is in the Westwood Industrial Area, only a mile or so up the main road from here. The pay isn't brilliant, of course. Fifty pounds a week.' He looked steadily at Tony. 'And he owes us six pounds fifty a week out of that. I'll tell you what, Mr Boyd. If he works well, we'll pay him six pounds fifty a week bonus – set off against the debt.'

'That's very generous of you,' said Tony. 'More generous than I could possibly have expected.'

'I haven't given him the job yet,' said Mr Widdowson, again with the slightly snubbing tone. 'If I do, it will, of course, be on account of you, and because of what you told me about the children. I must make that quite clear. I wouldn't normally risk employing such a man.'

He rose, with the air of putting an end to the interview. We shook hands formally and went out. In spite of Mr Widdowson's last remark, Tony was quite elated.

'It just shows,' he said, 'how little you can judge by appearances. People who seem cold and unfriendly can be as capable of generous actions as anyone else. I'm quite sure he means to give your uncle the job. Make certain he turns up at the right time, Kevin, clean and properly shaved, and it'll be all right, just you see.'

At Mr Widdowson's gate Dick rejoined us and Tony left, because he had to get home and finish preparing his sermon. Sandra hadn't spoken a word all through the interview, and now she turned to me and said:

'I didn't like him much, did you?'

'Who, Mr Widdowson? Oh, I don't know. You couldn't call him pally, but I suppose it's like Tony says, handsome is as handsome does.'

'But I don't trust him,' said Sandra.

'Why ever not?'

'Oh, just a feeling. Didn't you get it?'

This was not a silly question, because Sandra and I often

77

feel things in a similar way. I hadn't in fact felt any particular distrust of Mr Widdowson – mostly I'd been worrying about whether he would or wouldn't give Walter a job – but I had felt a very slight and subtle uneasiness, as if something was going on that wasn't altogether for our own good.

'Why should he go out of his way to help *us*?' Sandra went on.

'Because of what Tony told him,' I said.

Sandra took no notice.

'I'm sure Mr Brindley – you know, Mr Widdowson's manager, the one who called round about the payments – I'm sure he went straight round to see Mr Widdowson that night we listened at the hatch.'

'Well, what if he did? Mr Widdowson's his boss. Why shouldn't a man call at his boss's house?'

'No reason at all,' said Sandra. 'But he never came back, you know. We never saw him again. And next day Walter sold the furniture.'

'I don't know what you're getting at,' I said.

'Well, I do,' said Dick. 'Look, your uncle's been led into trouble before, hasn't he? What if Widdowson and Brindley are trying to get some kind of hold over him?'

'Oh, don't be so daft,' I said. 'What would they do that for?'

'They might want a cat's-paw for something.'

'You've been reading too many thrillers,' I said. 'Mr Widdowson's a city alderman. What would he want cat's-paws for?'

I thought Sandra might have supported me here. She is a down-to-earth girl, not given to wild imaginings like Dick. But now she said:

'Do you know what, Kevin? I felt once or twice as if Mr Widdowson knew all the time what he was going to say, and had it all worked out.'

'But how could he?'

'Tony told him on the phone beforehand why he wanted an interview,' said Dick. 'I expect he said enough for Mr Widdowson to put two and two together, if he really was interested in getting Walter into his clutches.'

It was all too dramatic for me.

'I don't believe it!' I said.

And at that moment a feminine voice said, 'Hello', and Anne Widdowson drew up beside us on her bicycle. She was carrying a tennis racquet and looking pretty good. I felt a flutter in my stomach.

Sandra and I both said, 'Hello.' Dick didn't say anything, because he didn't know who Anne was and I didn't know how to introduce them.

'I could give you that book now if you like,' Anne said. 'You know, the one I promised to lend you that day on Brightwell Crag. It won't take a minute.' And as I hesitated she went on: 'You could all come.'

But Sandra said, 'No, thank you,' and Dick still didn't say anything, and after an awkward moment I found myself walking back towards the Widdowsons' house with Anne while Sandra and Dick went on in the other direction.

As we walked up the drive, Mr Widdowson was just getting his car out. His eyebrows rose at seeing me again so soon.

'You know this young man, Anne?'

Anne smiled at her father.

'He's Kevin Thompson,' she told him. 'We met at Brightwell last week. Kevin, this is my father.'

'I've met Kevin already,' said Mr Widdowson. He smiled that wintry smile of his, and turned away. As he got into the driving-seat I noticed the smile had turned into a frown.

Anne looked curiously at me, and without telling her more than I had to, I explained that I'd been present at a talk about a job for my uncle.

'And did my dad help?' she asked.

'Yes, he fixed it up in no time. He was very kind, really.'

'He would be,' said Anne.

'I was doubtful at first,' I said. 'You know, he seemed a bit cool towards us.'

'Oh, that's only his manner,' said Anne. 'He goes to all kinds of trouble to help people. You've no idea.'

'It must be nice to be rich,' I said.

'Rich?' said Anne. She laughed. 'We're not rich, Kevin. Dad worries a lot about the business. Too many bad debts, you know, and he hasn't the heart to take people to court. And old stock piles up – once it's gone out of fashion you can't get rid of it. There's some dreadful old stuff at that warehouse.'

'Well, you seem rich to me,' I said, 'with your brother getting a car for his birthday and so on.'

'It's five years old,' said Anne, 'and he has to run it out of his allowance. Still,' she added contentedly, 'I suppose we're better off than most. My dad's great, really. We can talk to him about anything. And he does a lot of good.'

I thought of Dick and Sandra and their dark suspicions about Mr Widdowson. I hadn't really shared them, but I hadn't quite dismissed them either. Now I looked into Anne's eyes and I couldn't doubt that she was absolutely sincere. She thought her father was wonderful.

Half an hour later I left the Widdowsons' house with the book Anne had lent me. She hadn't suggested any further meeting, and I'd been too shy to do so. But I knew I'd see her again, because the book had to be taken back, and I would be careful to return it some time when I knew she was in.

I liked Anne. To tell the truth, I was rather taken with her. It was a new feeling for me. But I knew Sandra and Dick wouldn't want me to have anything to do with the Widdowsons. For the first time in my life I felt a conflict of loyalties.

9

My class teacher stopped me on the way out after school.

'I forgot to tell you, Thompson,' he said. 'Mr Reed wants to see you in his study right away.'

I went apprehensively down to the headmaster's study, which was on the ground floor near the main entrance. It had big windows and contemporary furniture and a carpet. Like the rest of the school, it was all very new and smart. But Mr Reed, the headmaster of Westwood Comprehensive, wasn't smart to match. He was a tallish gingery man in a gingery sports jacket, and he always spoke in abrupt Northern tones.

'Hang on a minute, lad!' he called when I arrived. He attended to a couple of teachers who had questions to ask him, then he signed a few letters, then he gave a very small boy a sharp talking-to. Then he told his secretary she could go. And then things quietened down, and he called me in front of him and gave me a long, shrewd look.

I felt myself trembling.

'Take it easy now,' said Mr Reed. 'I'm not going to eat you.'

He half smiled. He wasn't so bad really.

'Is this essay yours, Thompson?'

I recognized some work I'd handed in a few days before, and nodded.

'I'll come back to it in a minute. It's good. But first – you've got a brother in this school, haven't you?'

'No, sir,' I said. 'I've a cousin here, though. Harold Thompson, in 1A.'

'Harold Thompson, that's him. Listen, lad, I'm going to tell you something about this cousin of yours. He's a near-genius. Well, let's be on the safe side and just say he's brilliant.'

I thought with surprise of little knobbly-kneed Harold. We all knew he was bright, but we'd never heard words like that spoken about him before.

'You know what an I.Q. is?' Mr Reed went on.

'Yes, sir. It's how clever you are.'

'Something of the sort. Well, the average I.Q. in this school is about 95. Harold Thompson's is 170. It's pheno-menal. We've kept on re-testing him in case we'd got it wrong, but it's the same result each time. Going up a shade if anything. And Jim Lennox – Mr Lennox to you – has been trying this laddie with a spot of maths. Your cousin had never heard of algebra till a few weeks ago, but now he's got Lennox worried. Lennox knows the lad'll overtake him in next to no time . . .'

Mr Reed paused.

'You wonder why I'm telling *you* all this,' he said.

'Yes, sir.'

'Well, I wrote to the lad's father. And I sent him a reminder. But I haven't had any answer. So I made one or two inquiries. And I gather yours is – well, not the wealthiest of homes.'

I nodded.

'Now listen, Thompson . . . I'd better call you Kevin, or I'll forget which Thompson I'm talking about. Listen, Kevin, it'd be a crime to deprive this lad of his chance. You understand me, don't you?'

'Yes, sir.'

'Kevin, this boy's exceptional. There aren't all that many schoolmasters who are good enough to teach him. That's a new thought to you, I bet. But when you get a really bright lad you need a bright teacher to keep up with him. Well, there are just a few of them around. You know where you'll find them in this part of the world?'

Light dawned. I remembered the casual remark Harold had made at the bus stop some weeks before.

'Cobchester College!' I said.

'That's it. Dreadfully unfair, of course. It's all wrong that a few schools should grab the best of everything. But there it is. To make the most of young Harold that's where we'll have to get him.'

'But – ' I began. I thought of all the reasons why no member of our family could possibly go to a place like Cobchester College. There were so many that I didn't even know where to start.

Mr Reed went straight on without waiting. I realized that he was quite excited about Harold.

'Luckily,' he said, 'Cobchester College will take them at twelve-plus – if they pass a special exam. Mind you, it's a stinker, and the competition's enormous. They go on four things. An intelligence test – Harold's all right there. Mathematics – he'll waltz through it. Report from his school – leave that to me. Written paper – I'm not so sure, but there's nearly a month to go and we'll coach him for all we're worth.'

'But –' I began again. I still couldn't think how to explain the difficulties.

'There's nothing to pay, lad. He'll get a full scholarship. If he passes, that is.'

It was no good. I just couldn't bring myself to describe the characters of Walter and Doris. So I went off at a tangent.

'But would it be kind to Harold?' I asked. 'Wouldn't it cut him off from the people he knows, and set him among a different sort? Would he really be any happier?'

'A fair question, Kevin,' said Mr Reed. 'And I don't know the answer. In the end it depends on him. But I'll tell you this

– a talent like his needs developing, and Cobchester College is the place where they'll develop it.'

I said no more.

'That's Harold dealt with, for the moment,' said Mr Reed. 'Now, what about you?'

'About me, sir?'

'Yes. You'll be sixteen by the end of the school year. I suppose you've been thinking of leaving?'

'Yes, sir.'

'Got a job lined up?'

'No, sir.'

'Well, your work's good. Especially your essays. Not in the genius class, I'm afraid, but better than some. What about staying on in the sixth form?'

'I don't know,' I said. 'Things being as they are, I ought to start earning some wages. And I don't think my uncle would want me to stay on.'

'You don't know till you've asked him. Listen, Kevin, I want you to take this form home with you. It's an entrance application for Cobchester College. That's for Harold. Tell your uncle the whole story, tell him there's nothing to pay, and see if he'll sign it. If he won't, I'll call on him myself, but I don't like doing it – people sometimes say they've been put under pressure. And as for yourself, tell him I think you ought to stay on for two years. See what he says, and come back and tell me. Good luck, Kevin.

I went out with my head in a whirl. Mr Reed called me back from the doorway.

'You've missed the school bus, lad. What's it cost you to get home on the ordinary bus?'

'Fifteen pence,' I said.

'Here you are. Fifteen pence exactly. And don't you dare try to give me it back. What I want from you is that form, signed by your uncle.'

*

'Here he comes now,' said Doris.

'And about time, too,' said Sandra.

'We might have known he'd be late,' said Doris. 'An' today of all days.'

It was half past three on the afternoon when Walter was to see Alderman Widdowson about a job at the warehouse. But Walter had drawn his unemployment pay, and he hadn't been home for dinner. We'd all gone to the gate to look out for him.

'He's been in the Dragon again,' said Sandra. Sometimes I wish I could *hide* that place from him.'

'He'd find it, wherever it was,' I told her. 'And it's no good expecting him to pass a pub while he's got money in his pocket.'

'At least he's standin' up straight,' said Doris. 'That's something.'

'What's he doing now?' asked Sandra impatiently.

Walter had stopped half-way along Widdowson Crescent and was arguing about horses with Harry Brittain. Harry is a tall, lurching man in his late thirties. He is single and lives with his mother, who treats him like a child. Some say Harry is a bit soft in the head, though he can be quick enough at times. Now he and Walter were both talking at the tops of their voices and were probably being heard by everybody in the street.

'It was Joanna's Boy that won the Cambridgeshire, with Cecil Noakes up.'

'Get away, it was Cecil Noakes all right, but he wasn't on Joanna's Boy, he was on Moment Supreme.'

'Nay, it was the Cesarewitch that Moment Supreme won.'

'It was nothing of the sort. It was the Cambridgeshire. Moment Supreme won by a head.'

'He flippin' well didn't. It was Joanna's Boy . . .'

'Come on, break it up,' said Doris, pushing between them. 'You get yourself washed an' shaved, Walter

Thompson, an' get your suit on. Have you forgotten you're goin' for a job?'

'Here, listen, wasn't it Joanna's Boy that won the Cambridgeshire?'

'I don't know what won the Cambridgeshire,' said Doris.

'You don't know much, do you?' said Walter.

'I know you'll be late for that interview,' said Doris.

'Aw, flip off!' said Walter. 'I don't reckon much to that job anyroad.'

'Go on, Walt,' said Harry Brittain. 'You mustn't miss a job. They're scarce these days.'

'It's only because you know it was Joanna's Boy,' said Walter. 'You can't stand bein' wrong, can you?'

But Harry Brittain had turned his back and was continuing towards his own house.

Walter was persuaded not to follow him, and reluctantly came indoors.

'All right,' he said, 'all right. It won't do old Widdershins no harm to wait for a minute or two. Now, where's me dinner?'

'You haven't got time for no dinner,' said Doris.

'Well, give us some bread an' cheese, then.'

'Aye, well, you'd better eat something,' said Doris, 'if it's only to take that smell off your breath.'

'Gerr!' said Walter, and breathed hard into her face.

'An' you can get shaved an' put a collar on,' added Doris with unusual determination. 'An' then you can run like hell to the bus stop. An' even then you'll be late.'

Eventually Walter set off for the Westwood Industrial Area, wearing his suit and looking quite spruce. But he was a good quarter of an hour late, and there was still a faint smell of the pub about him.

'He'll never get the job,' said Sandra, and sighed. 'Well, honestly, if you were Mr Widdowson, what sort of an impression would that make on you?'

We had got a half-day from school, and it was a rather wretched one, because we spent most of it on tenterhooks. Sandra, as I'd expected, was eager for Harold to go to Cobchester College, and we'd decided that the best time to ask Walter to sign the papers would be after he'd got his new job. If he got it, of course.

Time crawled past. Five o'clock, quarter past, half past. With every minute that went by, Sandra and I grew gloomier. Surely if he'd been successful Walter would have come straight back. If he wasn't successful, he wouldn't show his face, and he'd probably spend the evening consoling himself at the Dragon. Gradually we became so pessimistic that we were actually startled when the door burst open and Walter came in beaming all over his face.

'I got it!' he announced. 'I got the job! Startin' on Monday. Fifty quid a week, plus bonus!' He gave Doris a friendly nudge. 'How's that, me old ruin?'

In dealing with Walter you have to take your chances quickly, before they disappear. I rushed upstairs to get the form Mr Reed had given me.

'What's all this?' Walter demanded. 'Cobchester College? What've we got to do with Cobchester College?'

'It's a special exam for Harold to take,' I said. 'He'd get a free place. And the headmaster thinks he's a good chance of passing it.'

'Our Harold at Cobchester College?'

Walter frowned. It was a difficult idea for him to grasp. I wondered if he would dismiss it outright. But Walter is always either up or down, and at the moment he was up. The beam broke out again.

'Did you hear that?' he said to Doris. 'Did you hear that? A lad of mine at Cobchester College!'

'If he passes the exam,' I added hastily.

''Course he'll pass it!' said Walter. 'Harold! Come here!'

Harold came sauntering in from the kitchen. Like his

father he is always either up or down. At the moment he was feeling pleased with himself, and inclined to be off-hand.

'Let's have a look at you, lad!' said Walter. 'Aye, he's got brains all right. Look at the shape of his head. Just like mine.'

'I suppose he gets his brains from you?' said Doris sardonically.

'Well, he must get 'em from somewhere,' said Walter with satisfaction. 'Now, Harold, you're not goin' to let your dad down, are you? You'll do right well in that exam, an' even better at school, eh?'

'I expect so,' said Harold, with a casual air.

'Well, you'd better. Cobchester College, eh? Cobchester College!'

'You have to sign this application form,' I said.

'I'll sign it,' said Walter. 'Give us a pen.'

I had a pen ready. Walter signed his name, slowly but with an elaborate flourish.

'And Mr Reed thinks I should stay on at school for two years,' I said.

'Two years more at school? You must be daft. You could be earnin' wages in a few weeks' time.'

I said nothing.

'When I was your age,' said Walter, 'I was glad to get out an' earn some money for my parents, to pay them back for all they did for me.'

I still said nothing, but Sandra broke in.

'If Harold goes to Cobchester College he'll stay till he's eighteen,' she said. 'Why not Kevin?'

'That's different,' said Walter. But he was in high spirits, and after a moment he said:

'You really want to stay on, Kevin?'

I nodded.

'Well, if you was to get a job, evenings and holidays, it might be possible. I'm not promising, mind you. I got a lot of responsibilities. But, I'm not against it. We'll see how we get on.'

He turned back to Harold.

'Here you are, lad!' he said. 'Here's something for you. Two quid. And another five if you pass that exam!'

'If you're handin' out money,' said Doris, 'you can hand some of it over here, because I need it, I can tell you.'

Reluctantly Walter pulled out what was left of his unemployment pay and pushed two or three notes across the table.

'Are we supposed to live on that till you get your first wages?' asked Doris in disgust. 'P'raps you think we can all go on to a diet of nice nourishin' fresh air?'

'It's all you're gettin'!' said Walter.

His tone of voice this time was less pleasant. I remembered that Walter's moods could change rapidly. So I slipped out with the signed form, went across to the Hedleys' house to beg a stamp, and put it in the post in time for the evening collection. Walter couldn't change his mind now without going to a good deal of trouble. I felt sure that even if he did have second thoughts about letting Harold try for Cobchester College he wouldn't get round to doing anything about it.

But for the next hour or two Walter still seemed to be delighted with Harold's prospects. We had sausages and baked beans for tea, which made it something of a red-letter day. After tea Walter said he was going round to give Harry Brittain the good news. And when he came back an hour later he was more pleased with himself than ever.

'He admits it!' he said delightedly. 'He admits it!'

'Who admits what?' said Doris.

'Harry Brittain. He admits it was Joanna's Boy that won the Cambridgeshire!'

10

'Flowers!' said Walter in disgust. 'Flippin' flowers!'

'Well, I keep tellin' you they didn't cost me anything,' said Doris. 'They gave 'em to Sandra at the greengrocers, seein' they was the last bunch and the shop was just closin'.'

'An' puttin' em in a jug in the window! What next?'

'Well, folks keeps walkin' past.'

'I'll say they keep walkin' past. They can't get past quick enough.'

'Now look here, Walter Thompson,' said Doris, 'it'd be more help if you was to do something yourself to make the place look respectable, instead of sniffin' at what I do. What about diggin' the garden? You saw that letter from the Corporation.'

'The Corporation can dig it theirselves if they're all that interested,' said Walter.

'What letter was that?' asked Sandra quickly. She always tries to keep track of things. But, of course, letters often arrive when we are at school.

Doris groped behind the kitchen clock.

'Here you are,' she said. 'It came on Tuesday, but your uncle won't take no notice.'

It was a duplicated letter on Cobchester Corporation headed paper, and it said:

Date as Postmark

Dear Sir/Madam,

It has been observed on behalf of the Corporation that no steps have as yet been taken by you to put into effect the cultivation of the garden at the premises in your occupation.

I am instructed to draw your attention to the fact that it is a condition of your tenancy that the garden be maintained to an adequate standard of cultivation to the satisfaction of the Corporation.

Unless therefore steps are taken by you to put into effect the said cultivation of the garden at the said premises within the period of one calendar month from the date of this communication, I am instructed to state that the Corporation will have no alternative but to consider the necessity of taking steps to bring about the termination of the said tenancy.

Yours faithfully,

(Squiggle)

per pro. Housing Manager.

Sandra wrinkled her brows.

'What does all that mean?' she asked.

'It means, if you don't dig the garden, they'll throw you out,' said Doris.

'It means nothing of the sort,' said Walter. 'They're just tryin' it on. You don't need to take notice of anything that comes from the Corporation unless it comes registered.'

'Well, it's time we did something about the garden anyway,' I said.

'You can if you like, I won't,' said Walter. The idea that I should do the work obviously struck him as a good one, and he went on:

'Do you good it would, a growin' lad like you to do a bit of work for a change. When I was your age they couldn't stop me workin'. My mum could hardly get me in for my meals. I was always makin' or mendin' something.'

'Blimey, how you've changed!' said Doris sarcastically.

'I'll go to Dick's and borrow a spade,' I said.

It was a fine Saturday morning, and I was feeling cheerful. Walter had been three weeks in his new job and was still going to work regularly. He was grousing a bit – there seemed to be some difference of view between Walter and his bosses on the subject of how hard a man should be expected to work – but that was only to be expected. Doris was keeping the house in fairly good order, and the two younger children were making a few friends. We were getting established in the neighbourhood. I knew that Sandra and Dick still hadn't got over their suspicion of Mr Widdowson, but I was convinced by now that it was nonsense. Certainly I wasn't going to worry about it on a day like this.

I got the spade, took it home, and started to dig. It was harder work than I'd expected. The soil was heavy and there was a fine crop of old bricks, to say nothing of nettles and scrubby grass. Work was going on in half the gardens of Widdowson Crescent that morning. Ours was by far the most backward.

I dug a couple of rows without attracting any attention, except from Mrs Bates, the mother of the two children who weren't allowed to speak to us. She commented to nobody in particular as she went past: 'And about time, too!' I worked on for a few more minutes and then Mr Farrow from No. 27 strolled round. He's a sporty-looking man who has a little girl and a little car and a little moustache.

'Nobody ever taught you to dig, did they, son?' he asked.

'I didn't know you had to be taught,' I said.

'There's an art in digging, like anything else. Look, starting on a new plot you want to take the turf off first. Stack it up in a pile to rot down, that's the secret. Here, let's show you.'

He rolled up his sleeves, took the spade, and cut a dozen neat turves. Then Harry Brittain lurched across from the other side of the street.

'What you tellin' the lad, Ted Farrow?' he asked. 'Don't take no notice of what he says, Kevin. It'll be wrong, you can bank on that.'

'You keep your big nose out, Harry Brittain,' said Ted. 'I'm starting him off the way he ought to go.'

They both grinned. Harry Brittain is well known for his readiness to argue with anybody about anything.

'You tellin' him to stack the turf?' said Harry. 'Waste of time. Dig it in, two spits deep, that's what to do with turf.'

'Full of couch grass, Harry. You don't want to dig that in, it'll come through.'

'Not if you do it proper,' said Harry.

Soon they were at it hammer and tongs. I just went on digging.

'We'll ask Mr Slater,' said Ted at last. Mr Slater lives at No. 11 and has a lovely garden – fit for a royal palace in miniature. Everyone regards him as the expert and treats him with great respect, especially as he is older than most of the householders in the district.

Mr Slater approached with due gravity. He wore gold-rimmed spectacles, a cloth cap, and a very long grey cardigan pulled down over his stomach.

'Good mornin', young man,' he said solemnly to me.

'Good morning, Mr Slater.'

'I hear there's some advice needed.'

'I was just telling the lad how to set about his digging,' said Ted Farrow. 'I told him to stack the turf. That's right, isn't it?'

Mr Slater nodded pontifically. 'A very good method,' he said. 'A very good method indeed.'

Ted pulled a face triumphantly at Harry Brittain.

'Well, I said he could dig it in instead,' said Harry.

Mr Slater considered the matter further, with his head on one side.

'Aye,' he said, 'aye. Well, that's all right too, so long as you sink it deep enough.'

Harry made a rude gesture at Ted.

'But which is the *best* way, Mr Slater?' asked Ted patiently.

Mr Slater was silent for some time.

'In my opinion,' he said gravely at last, 'in my opinion there's a great deal to be said on both sides.'

'Oh well,' I said, 'perhaps I'd better just get on with it my own way.'

'Look, it's not too late to put a few bedding plants in,' said Ted Farrow. 'I've got some French marigolds and lobelias left over. Just you clear that strip next to the path, and I'll bring them across.'

'Never mind his French marigolds,' said Harry. 'I'll give you something worth lookin' at. I've got some nice red an' white dahlias in the shed.'

Tom Williams from the other end of the street had wandered along by now.

'You want to finish diggin' it over before you start puttin' plants in,' he said. 'Use a bit of system, like.'

'Aw, go on,' said Harry. 'The lad wants to have something to show for his work, an' I don't blame him.'

'Instant gardening!' said Ted Farrow.

'Well, what do you think, Mr Slater?' asked Harry.

Mr Slater was lighting his pipe.

'There's a lot to be said for finishin' your diggin' first,' he said. He struck a match, cupped his hands round the bowl of his pipe, and drew on it several times. 'But there's no harm in havin' a few flowers to look at as soon as you can,' he concluded, puffing out smoke.

Mrs Robbins next door, seeing the conference in progress, had come to the wall with a tray. She smiled her pretty, uncertain smile.

'I thought you might all like a cup o' tea,' she said. 'Hot work, gardenin'.'

'Hot work gassin', you mean,' said Harry Brittain. 'Ta, duck.'

'A kind thought, Mrs Robbins,' said Mr Slater gravely, raising his cap.

'Saved my life,' said Ted Farrow.

I drank my tea quickly and picked up the spade.

'I'll go and look for those plants for you,' said Ted.

'Here, let's have a dig,' said Harry. 'Give us the spade, Kevin. You have a rest. Your turn again in a minute.'

'I've got a better spade than that,' said Tom Williams. 'Look, two or three of us'll soon shift some of the work. There's nothing like gettin' together on a job, an' that's a fact.'

A few minutes later the three men and I were all working in our garden, while Mr Slater sat on the low wall and puffed approvingly at his pipe. By the time I went in for dinner, the digging was well under way. No. 17 was catching up fast.

I took Anne Widdowson's book back on a fine Monday evening, soon after tea. I knew she was in, but I didn't know she was just going out again. I nearly turned back when I saw that David's red sports car was standing in the drive, with David at the wheel and a girl beside him. Anne was just getting in behind them, and all three were looking rather cross. But David and Anne both signalled to me to come on, so I went up and admired the car and was introduced to the other girl, who was called Margaret and had a posh accent. They were all ready to go out, and the reason why they were looking cross was that there should have been another boy, called James, and he had rung up at the last minute to say he wouldn't be coming. And having told me this Anne said:

'Kevin, we're just going a little run over to Brightwell. We thought we might have an ice or something at the Lakeview Restaurant there. Would you like to come?'

Now I was not really very keen to make up a foursome like this, and if I had known how to do it I would have declined with thanks. But I felt awkward and couldn't think quickly enough of a way of saying, 'No'. So before I knew what was happening I was sitting beside Anne in the back of the sports car and we were speeding up the Westwood Road.

It was not a very happy occasion for me. You had to speak quite loudly to be heard over the engine, and this embarrassed me, though it didn't worry the others. And they were all talking about people they knew, with Christian names like Charlotte and Simon, and of course I didn't know any of them. Then they got on to shows they'd seen, and I hadn't seen a show in my life. Then there was talk about riding horses and playing tennis, which were two things I hadn't ever done and didn't expect to. Anne tried to bring me into the conversation, but I couldn't think of anything to say that would interest them. So by the time we were sitting on the verandah of the Lakeview Restaurant, which was new and smart, eating fancy ices that David was paying for, I felt all on my own and pretty miserable.

Afterwards we all wandered down to the lake. David and Margaret walked briskly in front, and Anne put a hand on my arm to slow me down and let them get well ahead. And it didn't make me feel any better to realize that I was only in the party so that David and Margaret could be together without leaving Anne on her own.

I felt less happy to be with Anne than I'd expected. Not that I liked her any less. What bothered me was a feeling that we had only a little island of shared interest surrounded by a great big sea of differences. After a bit, the talk between us dried up, and we just walked on, not saying anything. I began to think that Anne was bored out of her mind, and I felt more unhappy still. Then we came to the landing-stage, where the attendant was still on duty and a few boats were tied up.

'Let's have a dinghy!' said Anne. 'You get an hour for one pound fifty.' And she added hastily: 'I've got the money.'

'A sailing-boat?' I said. I was alarmed. 'But I don't know how to sail.'

'It's all right, you needn't do anything. Look, you just sit there – that's right – and when I say, "Ready about!" you change to the other side and remember to keep your head down. That's all there is to it.'

'And what about the other two?' I asked.

'They'll see what we're doing. Anyway, they're not in any hurry. We needn't set off home for another hour.'

There was just enough breeze to keep the boat moving nicely. And Anne could sail it all right. Poised there in the evening sunshine with a brown arm on the tiller, she looked very much in her element. We didn't go straight along the lake but moved in a kind of zigzag because of the direction of the wind. After a while Anne said:

'Can you really tell stories, Kevin? Just making them up as you go along?'

I reddened, and wished Sandra hadn't mentioned this, the day we were on Brightwell Crag.

'Yes, I do it sometimes,' I said. 'Not so often now. The young ones used to like it, but I think they're growing out of it.'

'Tell me a story now.'

I was taken aback.

'I don't know where to start,' I said awkwardly.

'Begin like this. Once upon a time, on a summer evening, two intrepid adventurers set sail for regions unknown . . .'

'All right,' I said. That was enough to start me off, and I went on quite easily. After a while I realized I was telling a desert-island story, very similar to one I'd told to Harold and Jean the night when we sat alone in the old house in Orchid Grove after Walter and Doris had walked out on us. Similar but different, for although of course I didn't say so, in my own mind the inhabitants of the desert island were now Anne and myself, and we were having the most wonderful time swimming and lazing under blue skies and eating delicious fruit . . .

Anne said nothing except an occasional, 'Ready about'. She might not even have been listening for all I knew, though she smiled whenever I caught her eye. Just before our hour was up, we were recalled by signals from the landing-stage, where David and Margaret were waiting for us, and I realized with a start that it was getting chilly. I thanked Anne for the sail and she thanked me for the story, which seemed a funny thing to thank somebody for. I had a vague idea of helping her out of the boat, but before I could get round to it she had sprung ashore and was helping me.

Afterwards, going home in the car and listening to still more talk about the Charlottes and Simons, I couldn't quite believe in that hour on the water. It wasn't real, any more than desert islands were real. What was real was that we got back to the Widdowsons' house in Westwood Road and everybody said good-bye and nobody suggested any further meeting – at least, not with me. What was real, too, was that Dick Hedley was waiting for me just outside the Widdowsons' gate, and he wasn't looking any too pleased.

'Hey! Romeo!' he said sharply.

I reddened and walked on.

'Kevin! I want to talk to you!'

'All right, Dick!' I said. 'All right. I'm listening.' And I heaved a great big weary sigh.

'Kevin, you want to stop wasting your time hanging about after that girl.'

'I don't hang about. Anyway, what's wrong with her?'

'Nothing that I know of. But look, Kevin, she's got her kind of friends and you've got yours. Such as me, if you did but know it. And what's more, I still don't trust her father. I think he's up to something.'

'You said that before, Dick. I didn't believe you then, and I don't believe you now.'

'Well, I've almost got proof now,' said Dick.

'Go on, tell me,' I said. And I gave another weary sigh.

'Well, while you were chasing around in sports cars,' said Dick, 'I was up at Widdowson's warehouse.'

'So what?'

'And so was Mr Widdowson. And so was Mr Brindley –
you know, the fellow who came to your house.'

'Quite a party, eh?' I said sarcastically. 'What were you
doing there?'

'I only went up there to see how the land lay,' Dick said.

'Dick Hedley investigates!' I said.

'And I saw both their cars parked by the warehouse
entrance. Well, just inside the doorway and to the right,
there's a little office. So I crept up to the office door, to see
if I could hear them talking.'

'And could you?'

'No.'

I laughed, jeeringly. It was now Dick who was getting red
in the face, but he went on:

'I peeped through the window, though.'

'And what were they doing?'

'Going through columns and columns of figures,' said
Dick. 'And doing sums on separate bits of paper.'

'Well, I suppose that's the sort of thing you do if you're in
business,' I said.

'Maybe,' said Dick. 'But this is the thing. When they came
out, I slid off round the corner, but I heard Widdowson say to
Brindley, as plain as you can hear me now: "I think we've got
it all tied up, Joe." That's what he said: "I think we've got it
all tied up, Joe."'

'I expect they were talking about some business deal or
other,' I said.

'I bet they weren't! They were planning some piece of
dirty work. You mark my words.'

I got still more impatient.

'Listen, Dick,' I said, 'that's all daft, and you know it is.
Mr Widdowson's got pots of money and he's an alderman.
What sort of dirty work would he be planning? You've been
reading too many thrillers.' And then another thought came
into my mind, and I added:

99

'Or else you're jealous!'

This was a blow below the belt, but it went home all right, because as Dick admitted afterwards he hadn't liked seeing me in David Widdowson's sports car at all.

Seeing him wince, I followed it up.

'You're just trying to turn me against the Widdowsons, that's all!' I said.

This time I'd gone too far. Dick was furious.

'I'll give you a thick ear in a minute!' he said.

I thought he was going to do it, but he managed to restrain himself.

'Listen, Kevin,' he said, 'how long have you known me?'

I didn't know what made me answer, 'Long enough.'

'And have I ever let you down – you and Sandra and the kids? Have I ever let you down?'

'I'm not saying you have.'

'Then why can't you trust me? I don't know what's come over you, Kevin Thompson.'

'I've got a bit of common sense, that's all,' I said.

'You mean I haven't?'

Again I didn't know what made me reply the way I did. I heard myself say it, without it really seeming to be me at all:

'No, you haven't. You get dafter every day.'

'All right, Kevin,' said Dick. 'All right. I wash my hands of you. If things go wrong, don't come bothering me about it. That's all I've got to say. You go your own way. You keep on mooning about, if that's what you want. A fat lot of good it'll do you!'

And Dick stalked off. It was the first time I'd quarrelled with him. To tell the truth, I'd quite enjoyed it. It had given me a sort of glow of battle.

Five minutes later the glow had faded. I knew it was daft to fall out with so good a friend as Dick. But by then he was out of sight.

11

'Eighty quid I've won,' said Walter. 'Eighty quid on a one-pound treble. Rose of Tralee at three to one, then Riceyman Steps at evens, then Pick of the Pops at ten to one. Eighty quid! There's forecastin' for you!'

'Well, you've put plenty in the bookies' pockets before now,' said Doris. 'It was high time you won something for a change. Where's the money?'

'Harry Brittain went down to collect it for me. I'll pick it up from him this evenin'.'

'You can bring it back here. No goin' straight off to the Dragon, an' comin' home with the milk tomorrow mornin' an' nothing left.'

'Aw, flip off!' said Walter.

'You can give me ten quid to pay off at Lennards' for a start,' said Doris, 'then we can start shoppin' there again. And another ten for next week's rent. An' what about some shoes for Jean?'

'Go to hell,' said Walter, 'it's my winnings, not yours. Hello, Harold lad, where've you been?'

Walter's eyes lit up as Harold appeared. He had been extra proud of Harold lately.

'Been to tea with Derek Cutts,' said Harold.

'And who might Derek Cutts be?'

'Oh, just a friend of mine,' said Harold casually. 'He was top of the class till I came. Now I'm top. But he doesn't mind. They live in the private houses, the other side of Westwood.'

'That's a long way from here.'

101

'His dad ran me home in the car,' said Harold. 'They have a Volvo.'

'There y'are!' said Doris, as if this proved something to Walter's disadvantage.

'Must be nice having a car,' said Harold. 'They go all over the place. They often go to Brightwell in the evening. And up in the hills or even the seaside at week-ends. I wish *we* could.'

'You wish you could do that, eh, Harold?' said Walter.

'Yes, Dad, I do.'

'Some hope!' said Doris sarcastically.

'I don't see why my lad shouldn't have what others have,' said Walter.

'Don't you?' said Doris. 'Well, I do.'

'Here, Kevin, pass me that evenin' paper!' said Walter. He turned to the small advertisements at the back. 'Yes, I thought so.' With a pencil he made a big cross against an item he seemed to have seen before. And a minute later he went out.

Mr Hedley walked all round the small decrepit car that stood in Widdowson Crescent. Then he said:

'A fool and his money . . .'

Walter was unperturbed.

'It's cost me less than nothing, Jack,' he said. 'Two o'clock this afternoon I was skint. Then three horses come up, all in a row – eighty quid. Well, I've only paid sixty for the car. I've still got cash in hand.'

'You'll need it, if I'm any judge,' said Mr Hedley.

'Aw, get away with you!' said Walter. 'It's with being a motor mechanic. You can only think of what might go wrong.'

'Well, just look at it!' said Mr Hedley. 'Bodywork rusted right away round the bottom to begin with!' He tapped the offside door with his foot, and a few flakes of rust fell into the road.

'Here, go easy!' said Walter in alarm. And then: 'What do you expect for sixty quid? A new Rolls? So long as it holds together I'll be satisfied.'

'You'll have a right to be!' said Mr Hedley. 'What about the M.O.T.? It can't have passed that!'

'It has!' said Walter triumphantly. 'At the corner garage, down on Westwood Road.'

Jack Hedley frowned.

'They pass anything there,' he said, 'if you slip 'em an extra fiver. They'll be in trouble one of these days, I can tell you.'

'I should worry!' said Walter scornfully.

'Start up the engine, Walt.'

Walter got into the driving-seat. It took several attempts with the self-starter, and the battery sounded weary, but in the end the engine fired and blue smoke poured from the exhaust. Jack Hedley lifted the bonnet and listened for a minute, then raised his eyes to the heavens.

'Well, it's runnin'!' said Walter.

'Aye, it's runnin',' said Mr Hedley dryly.

'You reckon it wants anything doin' to it, Jack?'

'If you mean, am I goin' to do anything to it,' said Mr Hedley, 'the answer's "No". I wouldn't touch it with a bargepole. The state it's in, you'd best let well alone an' keep your fingers crossed.'

'I thought it might be worth gettin' a new set of plugs,' said Walter.

'Don't waste your money,' said Mr Hedley. 'That engine's not worth a set of plugs. Wipe the ones that's in it, Walter, carry a can of oil because it's usin' plenty, an' wherever you go, keep your bus fare handy, that's my advice.'

'Flamin' pessimist!' said Walter. He didn't seem worried. 'There, I'll take it on its first trip, down to the Dragon. Coming, Jack?'

'Got your licence and insurance, Walt?'

'I'll see about them on Monday.'

'Well, you can count me out,' said Mr Hedley. 'So long.'

He stood beside me as the car, still belching blue smoke, stuttered away towards the main road with Walter at the wheel. Mr Hedley groaned.

'If ever there was a man without any sense it's your uncle,' he said. And then, seriously: 'I hear you and Dick have fallen out.'

I was embarrassed.

'Sort of,' I said.

'Well, I'm sorry to hear it. Dick's a good lad. I'll say it even if I *am* his dad. You don't want to lose good friends, Kevin.'

I nearly told Mr Hedley what we'd quarrelled about, being sure he'd take my point of view rather than Dick's. But something kept me quiet.

'Well, come to us if you need us, just the same,' said Mr Hedley. 'Me an' Mrs Hedley'll stand by you – and so will Dick if it comes to the point.'

He patted me on the back. 'Good luck, lad. Take care of your Sandra. A gem of a lass she is, an' don't you forget it. Well, I'll be seein' you.'

I woke in the middle of the night to hear a strange, unearthly scream. It was followed by the sound of Walter swearing, then of thuddings and scrapings, then of the car chugging into our drive. And then I went to sleep again.

'Well, come on!' said Walter. 'All these years you keep moanin' that we never go anywhere, an' now we're goin' somewhere you're not so keen.'

'You think you're gettin' me in that?' demanded Doris.

'What's wrong with it?'

'Rickety old thing. It's only fit for the scrap heap.'

'It's not half as old as what you are!' said Walter. 'Maybe you're only fit for the scrap heap too?'

Doris muttered and grumbled. Sandra wasn't too happy either. But Harold's eyes shone. His imagination made good all the car's failings. To him it might have been the latest Jaguar. He couldn't wait to get out on to the road. And Walter was proposing a Sunday trip into the Pennines – the first family outing in all the years we'd been together.

'Oh well,' said Doris, 'heaven help us if it falls to bits, that's all. Harold, go an' get your things on. Jean, can't you stop snivellin'? The cat'll turn up, worse luck.'

Jean was in a bit of a state because Pussy hadn't come in for his breakfast. Her devotion to her battered tom-cat was as deep as ever. But the rest of us weren't worrying about Pussy – except perhaps Sandra, who didn't like to see Jean upset.

Soon the ancient car was chugging along Westwood Road, heading away from the city. Harold and Jean shared the front seat beside Walter, and the rest of us were squashed into the back. Walter, in good spirits, drove high on the crown of the road. Harold was full of excitement, but Jean sat silent and tearful, still thinking of Pussy.

Beyond the county boundary, where Westwood ended, we headed on narrow roads for the hills. A man in a faster car tried to overtake us, but Walter balked him for at least a mile. Finally, using the verge, he managed to get past, hooting furiously as he did so. Walter, delighted, stuck his arm out and made a rude gesture.

'We're not goin' up all them hills, are we?' asked Doris in alarm as the Pennines loomed nearer.

''Course we are!' said Walter.

'In this old thing? We'll never make it.'

This was the wrong thing to say. Walter took it as a challenge.

'We'll make it all right. We'd get up the side of a house in this car. Listen to that engine, it's runnin' lovely.'

None of us knew enough about the sound of engines to be able to argue. But I reminded Walter that Mr Hedley hadn't been impressed.

'Oh, Jack!' said Walter scornfully. 'Too cautious to live, is old Jack. It's with workin' at a garage. Half the work they do isn't necessary anyway – they only do it to take more money off the customer.'

The road was uphill now, but the old car chugged gamely along. Walter burst out singing:

'Oh we're off – on the road – to Morocco!'

'Be lucky if we get back home again, never mind Morocco!' said Doris.

'Aw, give it a rest for once,' said Walter. 'You're havin' a day out, aren't you? Be thankful. You might never get another. Now then, everybody happy?'

'Yes,' said Harold. Nobody else spoke.

'Well, it wasn't much of a chorus,' said Walter. 'Don't know why I bother with you lot. Next time, just Harold and me'll come, won't we, Harold lad?'

'Look, Dad! Look at that road up there, going right up the mountain!' said Harold.

I tried to shut him up, but it was too late. A narrow lane branched off from the main road and wound its way steeply up the hillside.

'Oh no, not that!' cried Sandra in alarm. 'Don't go on that one!'

'An' why not?' demanded Walter.

'You know why not,' said Doris. 'I don't mind you breakin' your own flippin' neck, but you don't have to kill the lot of us!'

'A fine pair of moanin' Minnies you are, you an' Sandra!' said Walter in disgust. 'You tell me, Harold, can we make it?'

''Course we can!' declared Harold.

Defiantly Walter swung to the left and set off up the steep

little lane. It wasn't really much more than a track. Soon he had to change into lower gear, then he changed down again, and after a minute or two we were crawling in bottom gear. Steam began to escape from round the radiator-cap.

'She's boiling!' I said urgently.

'Aye, well, maybe it *is* a bit steep,' Walter admitted. 'Never mind, we can't turn back now.' And it was a fact that the lane was too narrow to turn in, while reversing would have been a tricky proposition even for an expert driver. There was nothing to prevent a vehicle from going over the edge and straight down the hillside.

Clearly the poor old car couldn't carry all of us up the slope.

'You lot better get out!' said Walter after a moment. 'She'll go up like a bird if we get rid of the deadweight.'

He stopped. The handbrake didn't seem to have much effect, but Walter held the car steady on the clutch. Except for Harold, nobody was sorry to be safely out of it. Walter set off again, still in bottom gear, with smoke pouring from the exhaust and steam from the radiator. He travelled fifty yards or so before the lane turned a corner and became even steeper on its last stretch to the top. We watched from behind as the car ground slowly to a halt. When we caught up with him, Walter was again holding it on the clutch, with the engine roaring.

'Brakes aren't so flippin' brilliant,' he remarked. 'Still, we're nearly there now. If you lot get behind an' shove, we'll be over the top in a minute, then it'll all be downhill.'

'I'm not gettin' behind that!' snarled Doris. 'Suicide, that's what it is.'

I didn't fancy it either. If the car ran back, anybody pushing it might be under the wheels or over the edge of the road.

'Kevin! Sandra!' called Walter. 'Aren't none of you goin' to help?'

We still hesitated, but Harold piped up:

107

'I'll push, Dad!'

'Oh no you won't!' said Sandra. She took Harold by the shoulders and thrust him at Doris. 'Don't let him go!' she said fiercely. And then, with a look at me:

'Come on, Kevin, we'd better see what we can do.'

So Sandra and I pushed hard from behind, fearful that either the engine would stall or the whole thing would blow up. We were within a hundred yards of the top when at last it became clear that even with our help the old wreck would never get there.

I shouted to Walter, but he couldn't hear me above the roar of the engine. We pushed and pushed, ever more painfully. Soon it was taking all our strength to keep the car from running back. And then suddenly the driver's side door flew open and, yelling a warning to us at the top of his voice, Walter leapt out, abandoning ship.

'Won't even stay in flamin' gear now!' he said, shaken.

Sandra and I jumped aside. Doris and the younger children were luckily well out of the way. The car moved backward, slowly at first, then gathering speed, to the nearest bend. It lurched half over the edge, looking for a split second as if it was going to stick. Then the front tilted upwards, and down it went. Soon it was rolling over and over, and after a minute or so it came to rest in a field far below, with the wreckage of a drystone wall around it.

'You fool!' I cried. I could have hit Walter, I was so mad. 'You utter fool, you nearly killed us!'

Walter himself looked shaken, but only for a moment. Then:

'Come on!' he said. 'Let's get away from here, quick!'

'Are you just going to leave it there?' I asked unbelievingly.

'You bet I am! It's a write-off. And the transfer hasn't been registered, so there's nothing to connect it with me. Hurry up!'

Nobody seemed to have seen the incident except us.

Walter hurried us back to the main road. Doris luckily didn't realize what a near thing it had been, and was mainly concerned about the loss of money.

'Sixty quid!' she complained bitterly. 'Sixty quid, an' it hasn't lasted a day. That must be a record in chuckin' money away, even for you, Walter Thompson!'

Walter was recovering his self-possession.

'Easy come, easy go,' he said. 'I had nothing at this time yesterday, so I'm no worse off now than I was then. Might win another eighty next week, for all you know!'

'Might!' jeered Doris. 'That's a fine word. You might – an' you might not!'

'I'll have enough money by the end of this month to buy a real car, maybe,' said Walter.

'What do you mean?' I asked quickly.

Walter looked as if he'd been on the point of letting something out that he shouldn't.

'Nothing to do with you!' he said.

'Well, what do we do now?' asked Doris. 'Stuck here in the hills, ten miles from home.'

'There's a bus stop just down there,' said Sandra.

So there was, and there was a lady waiting at it. She told us we couldn't get a bus to Westwood, but we could get one to the centre of Cobchester. And the fare was sixty pence.

'And another twenty-five to get home from the city centre!' said Walter. 'Eighty-five pence. Blimey. It's a good job I took Jack's advice to carry my bus fare. Just enough for that an' the odd pint – that's all I've got.'

'An' what about us?' asked Doris.

'What about you?'

'Who's goin' to pay *our* fares?'

'You are.'

'Why, you rotten sod!' said Doris.

'Have you got enough?' asked Sandra quietly.

Doris groped in her bag.

'About three pounds,' she said.

'Well, that'll get you and the younger ones home,' said Sandra.

'An' what about you an' Kevin?' asked Doris.

Sandra's face was set in the thin, determined line that still reminded me of our mother, dead for five years now.

'We'll walk,' she said. 'Ten miles across country. It won't kill us.'

'That's right,' said Walter with approval. 'Do you good. When I was a lad there was nothing I liked better than a nice healthy walk in the fresh air.'

Sandra just looked at him, and even Walter wilted.

We got home, pretty tired, about five o'clock, and Sandra set about making the tea. Walter had gone out, which was just as well. During the long weary walk Sandra and I had not softened towards him, and it wouldn't have taken much to start a row between him and us. That would have been a new development, and not a very nice one.

Harold had gone to play with Leslie Robbins next door. Doris was depressed and bitter, Jean pale and tearful. Pussy still hadn't turned up, and Jean was more upset than I'd have thought possible over such an ugly beast. Between spreading jam on slices of bread, Sandra did her best to comfort the poor kid. And I was struck by a sudden thought.

I went out into the street and studied a stain that could be seen there. I fetched the spade that the Hedleys had lent me, and looked at a similar stain on that. Then I looked at a bit of the newly dug garden that seemed, on closer inspection, to have been dug twice. I wondered whether to dig that bit yet again, but decided not to bother. Considering what I'd seen just now and what I'd heard in the night, I knew beyond doubt what had happened. Walter's car had failed to injure any of us, but it had had a victim after all.

There was no point in saying anything to anyone. No point

110

in tackling Walter, no point in upsetting Jean still more. She would realize gradually, as the days went by, that she wasn't going to see her Pussy again.

12

'Funny little beggar, isn't it?' said Doris.

'He's lovely,' said Jean. 'Lovely lovely lovely. Come to your mummy, kit. You got a mummy, did you know, you got a mummy to look after you. *I'm* your mummy. Yum-m-m-m!'

Jean held the tiny black-and-white kitten between her hands, lifted it to her face and kissed it with passion.

'Dunno what your uncle'll say,' said Doris to Sandra.

Sandra had brought the kitten from Ted Farrow's house along the street. It was meant to comfort Jean for the loss of Pussy, and it was succeeding very well.

'My uncle put up with Pussy for all those weeks, so he can put up with a kitten!' said Sandra. She is getting increasingly bossy these days.

'Aye, well, it's only a little 'un,' said Doris. 'Bring us the milk tin, Harold. There's a bit left in the bottom. Here, cat, have a lick of that!'

The kitten put its head into the condensed-milk tin, and purred.

'He likes it!' said Doris, delighted. 'He likes it! What'll we give him to eat, Sandra?'

'I'll see to that,' said Sandra. As a matter of fact she'd been getting offal and fish-heads for Pussy from the Parade for weeks past, and the shops never charged her anything because they all knew Sandra.

'I'll make him a bed out of that cardboard box,' said Doris, 'an' we'll put him in the cupboard under the stairs at night, so your uncle won't tread on him if he comes in late. Ee, isn't he bonny! I'm fair struck with him.'

I couldn't ever remember seeing Doris so animated.

'What'll we call him?' she asked.

'That's for Jean to decide,' said Sandra.

'Kit kit kit kit kit!' said Jean, holding out a finger for the kitten to worry with its tiny paws. 'We'll call him Kit, of course.'

'He won't always be a kitten,' said Sandra.

'He'll always be Kit!' said Jean, with an air of decision. She went to sit on Sandra's knee, taking the kitten with her. 'I'm glad we've got him, Sandra, I'm ever so glad we've got him. You're glad, aren't you? Well, you must be, seeing you brought him. Harold, are you glad we've got Kit?'

'Oh yes, I suppose so,' said Harold, sounding a bit bored on purpose.

'And you're glad, aren't you, Kevin?'

'Yes, Jeannie,' I said. 'Yes, I'm glad we've got him.'

Jean looked at Doris uncertainly. Often it's hard to tell how Doris will respond. But Jean said:

'Are you glad we've got him, Auntie? Are you?'

''Course I am, duck,' said Doris.

'Then we're all glad we've got Kit,' said Jean with satisfaction. 'And I bet he's glad he's got us!'

Jean beamed. She was happy. Poor old Pussy was half forgotten already.

The letter arrived on the seventeenth of June. It was on crisp paper that crackled like a pound note, and the engraved address at the top was nothing more than 'The College, Cobchester'.

Dear Mr Thompson [it said]

I am pleased to say that as a result of our entrance examination

I am able to offer a free place at the College to your son Harold. All tuition fees and textbooks will be covered, but it will be necessary for you to provide uniform and sports wear. Term begins on 15 September.

We are holding a meeting for new parents at the College on Tuesday next, 23 June, at 8 p.m., at which we hope to answer some of the many questions which will no doubt occur to you. I hope we may have the pleasure of your company on that date.

Yours sincerely,

Denis Welby, Headmaster

'That's *Sir* Denis Welby,' I said.

'Blimey!' said Walter. 'A letter from a bleedin' knight!'

'Not just a letter,' said Sandra, 'an invitation.'

'Where's the lad?' said Walter. 'Where's my lad?'

Sandra ran to fetch Harold from the half-built houses where he was playing.

'Now, Harold lad,' said Walter, 'you listen to this.' And he read out the letter.

'Oh well, that's all right then,' said Harold casually.

'All right? I should think it *is* all right! You've won the scholarship!' Walter slapped Doris on the back, making her splutter over the cup of tea she was drinking. 'That'll show 'em all! My lad at Cobchester College!'

'I knew I'd win it,' said Harold. 'It was nothing. Dead easy.'

'Shows what Thompsons can do when they get the chance!' Walter went on. He was delighted with himself as much as with Harold. 'Now if they'd had things like this in my day I'd have won one just the same. When I was a lad they was astonished how brilliant I was.'

'First I've heard of it,' grunted Doris.

Walter's eyes were alight.

'Aye, I'd have shown 'em, if ever I'd had a chance. I might have been one of the bosses by now, instead of slavin' away like I do, with fellers orderin' me around. It's me that'd be givin' the orders. "Do this," I'd be sayin', an', "Do that," an', "Get a move on, can't you?" and they'd all be jumpin' to it.'

'Don't make me laugh!' said Doris.

'An' I wouldn't have saddled myself with *you*, I can tell you that!'

'Aw, stuff it!' said Doris.

'Can I go now?' asked Harold patiently.

'Aye, off you go, lad,' said Walter, and then: 'Here, half a minute!' He dipped into his trousers pocket and shovelled all his loose change into Harold's palm. 'My son at Cobchester College!' he said proudly, sticking out his chest and putting on an accent.

'It says you've to provide uniform an' sports things,' said Doris grimly. 'That'll cost a pretty penny to start with.'

'I'll not let my lad be short of anything!' said Walter with emphasis.

'Well, an' are you goin' to meet Sir Denis Thingummy?' asked Doris.

''Course I am,' said Walter. 'I'm not afraid of no knights. I'm as good as he is, any day of the week.'

Doris laughed jeeringly.

'Well,' said Walter, 'if he's got a lad, I bet he isn't no brighter than my lad, an' that's as good a test as any.'

He put on the accent again.

'Ay must just jot the engagement down in may diary, in case Ay forget, among all may other engagements with the nobility. June the twenty-third, sherry with may old friend, Sir Denis . . . Oh hell!'

'Now what?' said Doris.

'I'd forgotten – it's the night of the Civic Ball!' said Walter.

Doris thought he was still acting.

'You better wear yer ruddy evenin' dress, me Lord,' she said, 'an' then you can hop from one engagement to the other.'

114

'Nay,' said Walter, 'nay, I can't go to the school. I got something to do that night.'

'What is it?'

'None of your business,' said Walter.

'Something more important than Harold's school?'

'It's something that's got to be done on the night of the Civic Ball.'

'Well, go on, tell us what it is.'

'All I'm tellin' you is to mind your own business!' said Walter.

He looked sideways at Sandra and myself, and there was a furtive look on his face. It worried me.

'I'm sorry, Dick,' I said.

'All right,' said Dick. 'Apology accepted.' And he strode on.

'Dick, I want to talk to you!'

'Another time,' said Dick. 'I'm busy just now.'

'Let's go on being friends!' I said.

Dick said nothing but pointedly glanced at his watch.

'Look, I've told you I'm sorry!' I said.

'And I've told you I accept your apology,' said Dick coldly. 'But I haven't time to bother with you just now.'

I realized that he was still pretty cross.

'Dick!' I said. 'I think there *is* something fishy going on !'

'Is there?' asked Dick loftily. But he couldn't keep up the haughty tone. He was too interested.

'I told you there was!' he said. 'What have you found out?'

I explained that Walter had spoken two or three times of having plenty of money soon, and had mentioned something mysterious that he was to do on the night of the Civic Ball.

'I didn't like the way he talked about it,' I said. 'It sounded – well, suspicious. And, Dick, we just can't do with him getting into trouble again. Now that he's got a steady job and

115

Harold's going to Cobchester College, things are better than they've ever been. I'm scared stiff he'll go and spoil it.'

'If it's something shady he's doing,' said Dick, 'I wonder why it's to be done on the night of the Civic Ball. He's not going to burgle the Town Hall, surely.'

'Do you think it could be robbing somebody who'll be at the ball?' I asked.

'Well, that's a thought,' said Dick. We walked on in silence for a minute. Then:

'What's puzzling me,' he went on, 'is that your uncle isn't the man to plan a robbery or anything else. You know what I mean. He might just nick something on the spur of the moment, or he might take part in a job that somebody else had planned, but he'd never work anything out in advance for himself.'

This seemed true enough.

'I keep thinking of Widdowson and Brindley, and that remark about having it all tied up,' said Dick. 'I still wonder if he's in with them on something.'

'But, Dick,' I said – and this time I spoke very carefully, so as not to get him worked up again – 'Dick, you can't really think that Mr Widdowson and Mr Brindley would be planning a robbery. It just doesn't fit in.'

'Stranger things have happened,' said Dick. But after a moment he admitted: 'No, Kevin, you're right, it doesn't fit in. Not a robbery. Besides, if it was a matter of robbing somebody while they were at the Civic Ball I don't think there'd be a lot to be made from it, do you? I mean, nobody in Cobchester's terrifically rich. By the time you'd shared among three or more, it wouldn't be worth it.'

'I think,' I said – a bit nervously, because I knew the idea was firmly fixed in Dick's head – 'I think we might as well drop the thought of Mr Widdowson being involved.'

To my surprise Dick agreed. Perhaps he'd realized at last that his suspicions were too far-fetched.

'Well, then, let's start with your uncle,' he said. 'And it's not so difficult, is it, Kevin? We know the date of the operation, whatever it may be. Tuesday the twenty-third. All we've got to do is shadow your uncle every moment from when he leaves work that day until he goes to bed. If we've got it wrong and there's nothing shady, well and good.'

'And if he *is* up to something?' I said.

'Well, what we've got to do,' said Dick, 'is to prevent it from happening, whatever it is. After all, the main idea is to keep your uncle out of trouble.'

Dick sounded a bit wistful. He still has a romantic longing to play the detective and solve a major crime. Prevention is much less exciting.

'Listen, Kevin,' Dick went on, 'you'll be out of school before your uncle finishes work. You'd better be up at the warehouse by the time he's due to knock off. He might be going somewhere miles away, so you can't risk missing him. If you do have to go away from Westwood, you'd better ring Hodgsons, next door to us, whenever you get a chance, and they'll get me to the phone. I'll give you their number. But I should think most likely nothing will happen till later on, so if I haven't heard anything I'll come round to your house as soon as I can get away, and we'll keep watch together.'

Dick had spoken with growing briskness. He loves having something to organize. A born boss, that's Dick.

13

'Rose-bed over there!' said Dick. He pointed with a stick, like a general surveying a battlefield. 'Annuals in that bed next to the wall. Vegetables round that corner, where you won't see them from the house. And you could start a compost-heap just here.'

'Listen, Dick,' I said, 'I've had the advice of half the neighbourhood already, and everybody tells me different.'

That didn't worry Dick. He was drawing on the back of an envelope.

'System!' he said. 'That's what you need. System.'

It was the first time he'd been in our garden since I started work on it, and although we were really there to keep track of Walter, Dick didn't believe in wasting his time.

It was the evening of the Civic Ball. Walter had come home from work as usual, and was now sitting in the house with his evening paper. Doris had been nagging him a bit about not going to the parents' meeting at Cobchester College, but she hadn't nagged him very hard because she'd have been scared stiff to go anywhere near it herself.

'We'll just dig this bit here!' said Dick authoritatively, having finished the drawing to his satisfaction. And at least he was the kind of general who goes into battle with the troops, because he promptly started digging at a great pace.

It was half past eight when Walter came out of the house. He strode straight down the garden path, whistling cheerfully and not taking any notice of us.

We watched him walk along Widdowson Crescent to the corner of the main road. Then we sauntered along after him in an unconcerned, accidental kind of way. We could see before we reached the corner that Walter was waiting, with three or four other people, at the bus stop. When the bus came, we saw him go upstairs, and then we dashed up and got on board at the last moment. And of course we went inside.

Up Westwood Road went the bus, and past Mr Widdowson's warehouse. Two stops further along, Walter came downstairs and got off. He was the only passenger to do so, and if we'd got off at the same stop he'd have seen us and asked us what we were up to. So we let the bus get well away from him before leaping perilously to the ground. And heading back the way we'd come we were just in time to see Walter disappear into the Dragon Hotel.

Dick and I pulled wry faces. That probably meant another long wait. It wasn't nine o'clock yet. Closing-time was over an hour and a half away. And of course we couldn't go into the pub; all we could do was watch the entrance.

We took spells, so that it wouldn't seem too obvious that there were a couple of boys hanging round the doorway, but neither of us went far away. I'd never known time go so slowly. And gradually I began to think we were on a wild-goose chase. It struck me, as it hadn't done before, that Walter might have invented an imaginary engagement for this evening because he didn't want to admit to Doris that he too was scared of going to Cobchester College.

Dick would have none of this. His theory was that Walter had gone to the Dragon to meet his accomplices, whoever they were. Dick was itching to get inside. At last he went into the pub, pushed open the doors of the various bars as if he was looking for somebody (which he was) and got outside again before anybody could ask any questions. He looked slightly crestfallen when he came back to me.

'Your uncle's in the public bar,' he reported, 'and he seemed to be just talking about racing to a couple of fellows.'

'Did he look nervous – you know, all tensed up?'

'He looked a bit excited, perhaps,' said Dick. 'He was gassing away twenty to the dozen about horses.'

'He always gets excited about horses,' I said. 'I'm sorry, Dick, I reckon we're wasting our time.'

'No, I'm the one who's sorry,' said Dick, 'because I think he saw me. He looked across to the door at just the wrong moment. And I think he was startled then.'

'So he would be, if he did see you,' I said, 'because he knows you're under age.'

'Oh well, we'd better keep on waiting,' said Dick.

It was getting on for closing-time now. We heard the call for last orders, then lights were turned down, and the customers started coming out. Dick pointed out two men as the ones who'd been arguing with Walter about racing. They looked very harmless and ordinary, and they were still talking loudly about horses. Walter was no longer with them. It certainly didn't look like a conspiracy.

The flow of people leaving the Dragon slackened and stopped, and still there was no sign of Walter. After five minutes we began to worry a little. Finally a barman came to the door and was obviously going to close it.

'Is there anyone else inside?' Dick asked him, greatly daring.

The barman just shook his head and locked the door in our faces.

For a minute or two we were baffled. Then Dick said:

'There may be a way out through the yard. We ought to have thought of that.'

We went round to the back, where there was a walled-in area stacked with empty crates. It obviously wasn't a recognized entrance, but all the same it seemed quite likely that anybody who wanted to do so could get out this way.

'That's because I let him see me!' said Dick, accusing himself.

'I don't suppose it is,' I said. 'Anyway, what do we do now?'

Dick is never at a loss for long.

'Well, I think we'd have seen your uncle if he'd gone to the bus stop,' he said, 'and I think we'd have heard something if a car had picked him up. So perhaps he's still on foot. Let's head back along Westwood Road quickly, the way we came, and see if we catch up.'

It seemed a forlorn hope to me. But I couldn't think of anything better. So we trotted homeward along the

120

Westwood Road. And then we had a bit of luck, because we bumped into Harry Brittain, who was taking his dog for a walk.

'You haven't seen my uncle, have you?' I asked on the off-chance.

And to my surprise Harry Brittain said:

'Yes, I saw him just now, not far from the warehouse where he works. An' do you know what he said? He said, "You haven't seen me, Harry." Did you ever hear anything so daft? He said, "You haven't seen me, Harry," an' there I was lookin' him straight in the face!'

I was silently thankful for the slow-wittedness of Harry Brittain.

'Thank you,' I said, and we went straight on, at double speed. Obviously Walter had quite a start over us, for it was some hundreds of yards to Mr Widdowson's warehouse. And obviously too, that was where Walter had been heading. I didn't say anything to Dick, but I was now getting worried again. It would be like Walter not only to do something he shouldn't do, but to do it stupidly and get himself caught.

It was dark now, and we found it surprisingly hard to tell which was Mr Widdowson's warehouse, because there were at least a dozen long low buildings in the Westwood Industrial Area, and we'd never approached it from this side before. But after five minutes Dick said:

'I'm sure that's it, over there.' And then, almost at once: 'What's that glow in the end window?'

There was indeed a glow coming from the end window – no, it was coming from more than one window, it was coming from all the windows on our side of the warehouse, and it brightened as we got nearer.

'Oh no!' I said. 'For heaven's sake, not that!'

'It is!' said Dick. 'It's a fire!' And then:

'Look, there's a telephone-box just down the road. I'm going to ring for the fire brigade.'

And Dick was off at the double. He is always quick to act. But I thought at once about Walter. I wondered whether he'd set the warehouse on fire, and I wondered even more whether he was still around.

There was no door in the wall of the warehouse nearest to me. I ran round to the other side, away from the main road. There, the door was locked but a window was open. I peered in, but couldn't see anything except smoke and flames and an occasional shower of sparks. The fire seemed to be getting a grip rapidly. No doubt the stuff that was kept there – furniture and crates and packing materials – was highly inflammable.

I slammed the open window, with a vague idea of cutting down the draught and slowing the fire. Then somebody grabbed my shoulder. It was Walter, and he had obviously run up from behind.

'Clear off, Kevin!' he yelled into my ear. 'Get away!' And next minute he was clawing at the window I'd just closed. It opened again, and Walter began to squeeze through, going into the building.

It was my turn to yell at him.

'Don't be daft!' I shouted. 'It's suicide in there!' I tried to hold him back, but couldn't get a proper grip, and in a moment he was inside the warehouse.

I peered through the window again, but couldn't see Walter – only smoke. I shouted two or three times for him to come out. Then I got my lungs full of smoke and broke off, coughing. And at that moment Dick appeared beside me.

'It's – my uncle – in there!' I spluttered.

Dick pushed me aside, but I edged my way back. We both looked in. For a while we could see nothing but smoke. Then there was a sheet of flame inside, as something especially inflammable went up, and we both saw Walter. He was lying flat on the concrete floor, only a few feet away from us, and it looked as if he'd collapsed.

'With a bit of luck we'll get him out!' said Dick. 'I'll crawl along the floor to him. Don't follow me. Stay here, ready to drag him through the window!'

Dick had got his handkerchief out as he spoke, and now he wrapped it round the lower part of his face and swung himself in through the window.

I saw Dick drop to the ground and crawl away, then the smoke covered everything. The fire was getting a good grip now. It was making a fair amount of noise as the burning furniture crackled, and what with the heat and occasional flames and showers of sparks it was all pretty frightening.

I wrapped my own handkerchief round my mouth and peered in again. The smoke lifted enough for me to see Dick dragging Walter along the floor until he was directly below the window.

Then began the hardest part of the rescue. If it hadn't been a life-and-death matter it would have been funny. Walter was unconscious, and though not a heavy man was too much for Dick to pass up to me. It was like struggling with a sack of potatoes, but much more awkward. And Dick was getting distressed. Even down at floor level it was getting hard for him to breathe. It was growing hotter, too, and it could only be a minute or two before the fire reached this end of the warehouse.

At last I got my arms under Walter's, but I couldn't lift him out, and I had a moment's panic when it seemed as though I'd either have to let him go or be dragged inside myself. And then, mercifully, I felt somebody grab me round the waist while somebody else pushed in beside me to the confined window-space and got another grip on Walter. And next minute out came Walter, still unconscious of course, and he and I and the two men who'd come to the rescue were all in a heap on the ground.

'There's one still inside!' I yelled, trying to disentangle myself. One of the men was back at the window before me,

123

and Dick, now at his last gasp, the handkerchief lost from his face, was dragged headlong into the open air and flopped to the ground. He lay there taking great gulping breaths. It was a minute or two before he could even grin at me.

A dozen or more people had now arrived, and most of them were gathered round Walter. He looked an alarming sight: his face blackened and bleeding, his clothes torn and charred. But at least he was still breathing.

A light van came backing up to us, and Walter was lifted into it.

'You two lads had better come as well,' somebody said. 'We'll be at Westwood Hospital in less time than it'd take to get the ambulance out!'

I felt weak in the legs, and had to be helped in through the back door of the van. Dick was recovering rapidly, but he too seemed a bit shaken, which wasn't surprising as he'd done much more than I had. As the van turned into Westwood Road it met the first of the fire-engines, and three more of them passed us before we got to the hospital.

They treated Dick for two or three bruises and a slight burn, and both of us for shock, and then they said we could go home, but Walter was to stay in hospital overnight. He had come round and there was nothing seriously wrong with him. The man with the van had waited for us, and by the time we left the hospital he'd been joined by a reporter – a very young man of about eighteen with a quiff of blond hair falling over his forehead who kept saying something about 'making all the nationals'. An equally young photographer was with him. Dick and I explained how we'd been passing by and had seen the fire in its early stages, but of course we didn't say why we were there. I told the reporter truthfully how Walter had come running up out of the darkness and had insisted on diving in through the window.

'I suppose he went in hoping to fight the fire?' the reporter asked, and I said I supposed he did. And I gave as clear an account as I could of how we'd seen him on the floor, how Dick had gone in after him, and how with the help of the two men who arrived later we'd dragged Walter out.

I was feeling dazed and tired by now, and it was getting late. The van owner took us back to Dick's house, and the Hedleys insisted that I should stay there overnight while they sent a message round to Doris. I slept for a long time, but uneasily, because I dreamed again and again that I was trying to drag Walter out of that window, always without any success.

It wasn't until the morning that I realized we were all heroes. Then Mr Hedley came in with the *Daily Echo*. It was the northern edition, printed in Cobchester itself, and the story was all over the front page. There was a huge picture of the warehouse on fire, with firemen directing jets of water on to it. There was a flashlight picture of Dick and myself, white-faced and staring, and looking like a couple of halfwits. And a third picture was of Mrs Hedley: 'So proud, says grey-haired mother.'

And the story!

BOYS SAVE THE MAN WHO FOUGHT
£160,000 BLAZE

said the main headline. I couldn't read it without blushing. It was clear that Walter was a hero for trying to put out the fire single-handed, and Dick and I were heroes for rescuing him. There were interviews with both our families and with Mr Widdowson ('Boss called from Civic Ball', said a subsidiary heading) who expressed his horror at the event but his gratitude to Walter.

Dick stayed off work, and I had a day off school, and what a day it was. Reporters and cameramen were still following up the story. About dinnertime they took Dick and me round to our house and posed us on the steps to meet Walter as he was brought home from hospital. Mr Widdowson was there too, and a television camera team, and everybody shook hands with everybody else, and Walter sat up feebly on the stretcher and said that he'd only done his duty but that Dick and I were magnificent.

Next morning Walter sent Sandra out early to buy all the papers, and it was still quite a prominent story, though it had moved to the inside pages. Walter was delighted and read long extracts aloud. Doris was bemused by the whole affair and quite unimpressed by Walter's heroism.

'Always up to something daft,' she said, 'an' just because it seems to have turned out all right this time you'll be thinkin' you can do something even dafter . . .'

But Walter shut her up. Myself, I was most glad of all to read a paragraph which the papers had tacked on to the story almost as an afterthought. The cause of the fire, it said, was believed to have been an electrical fault.

14

The second day after the fire, things began to look less rosy. The police, who had previously paid a brief visit and spent most of it congratulating Walter, now came back looking stern, and turned everybody out while they interviewed him for upwards of an hour. And when they left Walter was looking pale.

'Flippin' coppers!' he said. 'They'd shop their own grandmothers if it helped 'em get promotion. Tryin' to make out it was me that started the fire now.'

'An' did you?' asked Doris.

'I've told 'em I didn't,' said Walter, 'an' I'm stickin' to it.

Trouble is, they found that old lighter of mine just by the spot where they think the fire began. But I keep pointin' out to them, if you work at a place, you can easy drop your lighter anywhere. It doesn't prove a thing.'

That evening the police came again. It was my turn to be questioned. I gave them all the facts, but I didn't tell them about the suspicions that Dick and I had had. The next morning they were back once more. After a long interview Walter went with them to the police station. He returned looking very gloomy indeed.

'I've to go again first thing in the mornin',' he said. 'And I can tell you what's comin'. They'll be chargin' me, an' they'll whip me straight off to the city magistrates' court an' get a remand pendin' further inquiries. That's what they'll do.'

'Let's ring up Tony Boyd and tell him about it,' I suggested.

'What, that parson feller? I don't see much point. Anyroad, I reckon it was him as much as anybody that got me into this mess, by gettin' me the job in the first place. No, what I'm doin' is goin' round this evenin' to see Mister Alf Widdowson.'

And after Walter had had his tea he stumped grimly out of the house. Half an hour later he was back, white-faced and furious.

'The rotten so-an'-so won't see me,' he said. 'Sent a message that he'd had some information from the police an' thought he'd better leave the matter in their hands.'

'You'll let me ring Tony Boyd now, won't you?' I said.

'Oh, I suppose so. I still can't see that it'll do much good,' said Walter dispiritedly.

I was on my way round to the Farrows' house, where there was a telephone, before he'd finished speaking.

*

'Camellia 2491,' said Tony's voice.

'Hello, Tony,' I said. 'Kevin here. Kevin Thompson.'

'Why, hello, Kevin! How did you know?'

'Know what?'

'Sheila's had her baby today. It's a boy. They're both fine!'

'That's terrific, Tony!' I said. 'Congratulations.'

I'd have been more enthusiastic if I hadn't been so worried.

'What are you calling him?' I asked.

'I think we'll call him Peter. He weighs seven and a half pounds, and he's got blue eyes and fair hair . . .'

And Tony told me all about his son. You'd have thought it was the only baby there'd ever been. He was thrilled to bits. It was a shame to bother him with our troubles on such a day. But I hadn't any option. I told him everything I knew.

'Oh, golly!' said Tony. 'I thought I'd done so well, getting your uncle a job at Widdowson's. And now he's set fire to the place, eh?'

'He says he hasn't,' I pointed out.

'And what do you think, Kevin?'

'I don't think anything,' I said. 'Except that I think it would help if you could come out here first thing in the morning.'

I don't suppose Tony was terribly keen to come out to Westwood again, but he never hesitated.

'I'll be there, Kevin,' he said.

But, as it turned out, it didn't help much, after all. Walter had been quite right about what was going to happen. He appeared in the city magistrates' court, charged with maliciously setting fire to Mr Widdowson's premises. The magistrates granted him legal aid and deferred the case for a fortnight. Tony would have gone bail, but there was a snag. Walter had once been given bail before, and had failed to turn up when he should have done. The police had had to collect him from a neighbouring town. So this time they opposed bail, and the magistrates upheld them.

Walter was remanded in custody.

When Sandra and I got home at teatime it was obvious that everybody in Widdowson Crescent knew what had happened. Little groups of people melted discreetly away into their houses as we approached. Sandra stalked along like a queen, her head high in the air, looking neither right nor left.

Doris was buttering bread. Harold and Jean had caught an earlier bus and were home before us.

'I got a bit of potted meat for us,' Doris said. 'Mash the tea, Sandra, will you?'

'It happened, then,' I said.

'Oh, aye, it happened,' said Doris. 'Remanded to the Assizes. I wonder what he'll get.'

'Who says he's guilty?' asked Sandra coldly.

'Oh, he did it,' said Doris. ''Course he did it. He says he didn't, you know, he even said that to me, but I know him. He did it all right. Where's the kitten? Give him that tin to lick out, Jean love.'

'Well, what do we do now?' I said.

'What *can* we do?' asked Doris. She said it so indifferently it was hardly a question at all.

'We can manage,' said Sandra, 'if we try. Anyway, he might be acquitted.'

'Some hope,' said Doris. 'Harold, you want another butty? Pass us the knife, then, or you'll be cuttin' yourself.'

Jean piped up. She didn't know what it was all about, but she realized that there was a crisis. And she put straight into words what had been in Sandra's mind and mine.

'Are you staying, Auntie?' she asked.

Twice before when there'd been trouble in the household,

Doris had walked out. She'd come back both times, it was true – once of her own accord and once under pressure from Tony and Sheila. But we didn't feel too sure of her.

Doris didn't reply for a minute. She was buttering bread mechanically. Then she turned her slow, heavy look on Jean.

'I reckon I'll be stayin',' she said. 'I don't know where else I'd go.'

There was another minute's silence, and then Doris added, as if surprised by her own thoughts:

'I don't know what you'd do either, you four and the cat.'

This was the first time in all the years I'd known her that I ever heard Doris express the least interest in what happened to us. It was hardly believable.

'We'll have to go on social security,' Doris went on. 'It isn't the first time. Mean lot of beggars they are. Don't give you enough to live on, not properly. Seem to think you can spend your life boilin' bones for soup.'

'I can earn something,' said Sandra. 'I can sew and wash and baby-sit.'

'I can leave school next month,' I said. And it was true, because I would be sixteen in three weeks' time and the school year was nearly over. I didn't have to stay on.

'Oh, aye,' said Doris. 'Well, I had my doubts about you stayin' on, anyway. You're plenty old enough to start earnin'. When I was a lass we left school the day we was fourteen, an' that was that.'

'There's no need for Kevin to leave,' said Sandra in her sharpest voice.

'Well, it's up to him,' said Doris indifferently. 'I expect we'd manage somehow.'

'At least you needn't decide till we hear the verdict,' said Sandra to me.

There was a tap at the door, and Mrs Robbins put her pretty, anxious face round.

130

'Oh, you've started your teas,' she said. 'I was just thinking about your Harold. Him and Leslie play so well together these days, I thought he might like to have his tea with us, regular. I mean, when I'm making tea for three, it's no more trouble to make it for four, is it?'

She looked anxiously from Doris to Sandra, wondering what reception the idea would get. I wondered, too, knowing Sandra's pride and Doris's resentment of interference.

But things were changing at 17 Widdowson Crescent. Doris swallowed and said:

'It's right kind of you, Mrs Robbins, I'm sure. Harold, would you like that?'

'Ooh yes,' said Harold. 'They have ham and salmon and all kinds of things, don't you, Mrs Robbins?'

Sandra stared thin-lipped out of the window and said not a word. I knew it was a hard moment for her. She can't bear to be indebted to anybody. Mrs Robbins looked at her and back to Doris, and the uncertain smile flashed out.

'Well, we have to help each other, don't we?' she said. 'I mean, we never know when we'll need help ourselves, do we?'

'*You'll* never need it,' said Doris with momentary bitterness, and then, recovering:

'Harold, say thank you to Mrs Robbins for being so kind to you.'

'Thank you, Mrs Robbins,' said Harold dutifully. 'Can I come round now?'

'You've had your tea!' said Sandra sharply.

'I expect he can do with a bit more. They can always eat a bit more at that age, can't they?' said Mrs Robbins. 'Yes, you come now, Harold love. Leslie'll be looking forward to seeing you.'

'Has he been givin' you any – you know, trouble?' inquired Doris. 'I mean, you haven't missed anything lately?'

Mrs Robbins looked shocked.

'Oh, no,' she said. 'Harold's as good as gold these days. He seems to have more faith in himself. You know what I mean? It must be with winning that posh scholarship.'

'It's hard lines about that,' said Doris when Mrs Robbins had gone. 'He'll never be able to go to Cobchester College now. We just couldn't manage it.'

'Uncle's not been found guilty yet,' said Sandra. But Doris just shrugged her shoulders at that.

'He'll go to Cobchester College if I know anything about it!' I said. And I meant it. Perhaps I ought to have felt right down in the dumps, but at that moment I was suddenly full of determination.

'Well, queerer things than that have happened,' said Doris. I could tell she didn't feel like arguing.

'Jeannie,' she went on, 'you can give the cat them bits of potted meat that's left. See if he likes 'em. He'd better – it's fancier food than we'll be gettin' ourselves for a bit.'

15

It was a wet, dreary day when Walter's case came up for hearing at Cobchester Assizes. The magistrates had committed him for trial, and Dick and I were summoned to attend as witnesses. For nearly an hour we sat side by side on a bench in a dingy little room, waiting to give our evidence. I hadn't seen Walter since his remand in custody, but Tony had told me he was still claiming to be innocent.

It was like waiting for the dentist, but worse. I was sick inside with worry. We were joined first by a tall, silent grey-haired man, and then by Alderman Widdowson, who looked at us coldly and didn't say a word. I was glad when I was the first to be called, and found myself being led into court.

There was no mistaking the Judge, who was raised above the court and wore a full wig. I knew who he was. He was Mr Justice Burton, and Tony had said he was one of the younger judges, though he didn't look specially young to me. He wore spectacles and was writing busily with a fountain-pen. He didn't look up as I went into the witness-box. I could see Walter in the dock – a small, lonely figure who grinned nervously when I caught his eye. The jury were all men, except for one middle-aged lady. In front of the court, facing the Judge, was a row of gentlemen in black jackets and short wigs. Obviously they were the barristers.

I was asked my name and age, and whether I understood what the oath meant. When I said I did, I had to put my hand on the Bible and swear that I would tell the truth, the whole truth, and nothing but the truth. And then one of the gentlemen in short wigs stood up to ask me questions, and I knew he must be the prosecuting counsel.

I knew who he was, too, because Tony had told me. He was Mr J. C. W. Rimington. He wasn't actually a Q.C. Tony had said he was a junior, but like the Judge he didn't look very junior to me. He had a round pink face and was very nice and polite. He called me by my first name, and he said everybody knew it was rather an alarming occasion for me, but I didn't need to worry and they weren't trying to trip me up. All I had to do was just give straightforward answers to his questions and I would be all right.

So I explained how Dick and I, walking along Westwood Road that night, had seen what looked like the beginning of a fire, how Dick had gone to ring the fire brigade, and how Walter had come running up and dived in through the warehouse window. And then of course I told the story of the rescue, and Mr Rimington said it had been a very brave performance. And I was just thinking that everything was going quite well, and that nothing I'd said could have done Walter any harm, when the Judge leaned forward.

'What I haven't quite understood, Mr Rimington,' he said – and he said it in a beautiful voice, so that it sounded like poetry – 'what I haven't understood is how these two boys came to be on the scene at exactly the crucial moment.'

'I was about to ask him that, my Lord,' said Mr Rimington. 'Kevin, why were you and your friend walking along Westwood Road at that particular time? What time was it, by the way?'

'It was just after closing-time,' I said. There were one or two titters, and I wondered if somebody would shout, 'Silence in court!' but nothing happened.

'And why were you in Westwood Road at that time?'

'Well, we were just walking along there – '

'So you have told us,' said Mr Rimington patiently, 'but why?'

'Well . . .' I began, and stopped. I'd have liked to say that Dick and I had just been going for a walk, but I remembered I'd sworn to tell the truth and I didn't know what to do.

Then the Judge leaned forward again.

'Kevin,' he said, 'were you *following* your uncle?'

This hit the nail on the head all right. I could only nod my head and say faintly:

'Yes.' I didn't dare to catch Walter's eye.

'And why were you following him?' asked Mr Rimington.

I licked my lips. My mouth felt very dry.

'Well . . .' I said yet again. Even if I'd known what to answer, I didn't feel as if I'd have been able to say it.

'You must try to help the court, Kevin,' said Mr Rimington, still in a patient voice but with a slight edge to it.

'We thought he must be up to something,' I said limply.

'Such as what?'

134

'Well, we didn't know. It was just a feeling we had.'

'And what gave you this feeling?'

I was at a loss again, and didn't say anything.

'Was it something he'd told you?'

'Oh, no,' I said.

'But there must have been some reason . . .'

'Well, he said he was going to be busy that night,' I said miserably, with a feeling of letting Walter down, 'and I didn't want him getting into trouble when things were going well.'

'He didn't say in what way he was going to be busy?'

'No.'

'But you thought if your uncle was busy that meant trouble?' asked Mr Rimington.

Here another gentleman in a wig got up, but before he could say anything the Judge stepped in.

'I think, Mr Rimington,' he said in his beautiful voice, 'we had better leave it at that. The question is hardly admissible.'

Mr Rimington looked a bit put out.

'In that case, my Lord,' he said, 'I have nothing more to ask this witness.'

The gentleman who'd got up a moment ago rose to his feet again. I knew he must be the defending counsel, and was therefore Mr B. H. Goodwin. He was quite a lot younger than either the Judge or Mr Rimington, with a thin, sharp but likeable face, and he grinned at me reassuringly.

'The fact is, Kevin,' he said, 'that you were just acting on a vague hunch, and you had no concrete reason to suspect anything whatever?'

'That's right,' I said, relieved. At last I dared to look at Walter, who was gazing gloomily at nothing in particular.

'And let's get this clear. You didn't see your uncle going either into or out of the warehouse until it was already well on fire?'

'No, I didn't.'

'And you are quite clear that he came running up to the warehouse from somewhere else?'

'Yes.'

'So you naturally assumed he was trying to stop a fire rather than start one?'

'Yes, sir,' I said.

'That's all, my Lord,' said Mr Goodwin, and he grinned at me again as he sat down. I felt a bit better as I left the witness-box to sit in the body of the court beside Tony, who was there as a member of the public. After all, the plain facts were what Mr Goodwin had just brought out, and they were to Walter's advantage. I felt better still when Dick came to the witness-box, confirmed what I'd said in every detail, and wasn't asked anything about his suspicions.

But I didn't feel so happy when the next witness gave his evidence. This was the tall man who'd sat in the waiting-room with us. He turned out to be some kind of expert on fires, and he said that the electrical fault that was first thought to have caused the outbreak couldn't in fact have done so.

'Then how do you think this fire was started?' Mr Rimington asked.

'I think it was probably started in the good old-fashioned way, with a light and a splash of paraffin.'

After this came a detective-sergeant, who made things look even worse for Walter by producing the ugly home-made cigarette-lighter that Walter had made for himself one time when he had a job at a Royal Ordnance Factory. It was found, the sergeant said, close to the place where the fire had begun, and so was a can that had contained paraffin.

Up to this moment I'd been hoping that Walter really was innocent, as he had claimed to be. Now things began to look black. I found it hard to believe that even Walter could

136

have been so stupid as to leave a cigarette-lighter and paraffin-can on the spot where he'd started a fire. But apparently that was what he'd done.

Alderman Widdowson was called next. My heart sank as he stepped into the witness-box. Mr Widdowson said that as usual he'd called at the warehouse on his way home, just after half past five, to check that everything was in order. He was in fact the last person to leave the place on that particular evening. He'd left all the doors and windows locked, and there were no electrical appliances switched on. He had no reason to think that anything was amiss.

Then Mr Rimington asked how long Walter had been on his staff.

'About six weeks,' said Mr Widdowson.

'And how did you come to employ him?'

'I was asked to do so by a Mr Boyd – the Reverend Mr Boyd – who is Vicar of St Jude's in Cobchester. I gathered that Mr Boyd wanted to help this man, who had been going through a difficult patch.'

'And was Thompson a satisfactory employee?' asked Mr Rimington.

'To be frank,' said Mr Widdowson in his cool, smooth tone, 'he was by no means satisfactory. I kept him on because I didn't want to disappoint Mr Boyd by appearing to dismiss him before he had had a fair chance. But I couldn't have kept him much longer.'

'What was wrong with him?'

'A lazy man,' said Mr Widdowson. 'A poor timekeeper, a constant grouser, sullen and sometimes insolent. Moreover, as the weeks went by I formed the impression that he had developed some kind of grudge against me.'

Walter, who now looked half puzzled and half angry, was gripping the sides of the dock with both hands.

'And have you any idea,' Mr Rimington asked, 'why this man should bear a grudge against you?'

'I have no idea,' said Mr Widdowson, smiling faintly. 'I had done him nothing but kindness. There was a little matter of arrears of payments in which I was able to help him. I can only think that he may be one of those people who have an irresistible urge to bite the hand that feeds them.'

'That's a lie!' shouted Walter from the dock. He was promptly told to be quiet.

Now it was Mr Goodwin's turn to question Mr Widdowson.

'Mr Widdowson,' he said, 'although you had formed the impression that Thompson had some kind of grudge against you, you did not in fact suppose that he would do anything so wicked as to fire your warehouse?'

'I did not,' said Mr Widdowson. 'Frankly, I could not have imagined any such thing.'

'When you first heard about the fire, what were you told?'

'I was told that Thompson had tried unsuccessfully to put it out.'

'And what was your reaction to that?'

'I was surprised, but I thought "Good for Thompson". I thought I must have misjudged the man.'

There was no doubt that Mr Widdowson was an impressive witness. He spoke calmly and firmly, like a man who was used to being listened to with respect. And he showed no sign of malice.

'And when you learned that the fire was believed to have been started deliberately,' said Mr Goodwin, 'what was your reaction?'

'I could hardly believe it.'

'Would you ever have thought Thompson was the man to commit a crime on this scale?'

'No,' said Mr Widdowson, 'I would not – until now.'

The last two words, quietly spoken after a moment's pause, carried terrific conviction. My heart sank as Mr Goodwin sat down, having finished his cross-examination. I decided that Walter's chances weren't worth tuppence.

'My Lord, that completes the case for the prosecution,' said Mr Rimington.

'Well, Mr Goodwin?' said the Judge.

'I shall call the defendant as my first witness,' said Mr Goodwin.

Walter went from the dock to the witness-box and took the oath. Mr Goodwin was watching him closely and didn't look at all happy. I could guess what was in Mr Goodwin's mind, because it was in mine, too. If ever there was a man with the knack of being his own worst enemy, it's Walter. His manner now was nervous but aggressive. Mr Goodwin seemed to spend a good deal of time on unimportant preliminary questions, and even I could see that the idea was to calm Walter down.

'And where did you spend the evening of the twenty-third?' asked Mr Goodwin, when at last he got to the point.

'I was in the Dragon, having a pint or two,' said Walter.

'When you say a pint or two,' said Mr Goodwin, 'you mean just that? In plain English, were you sober when you left?'

'Sober as a judge,' said Walter, and again there were one or two titters, but nobody thought it worthwhile to do anything about them.

'And after you left the Dragon where did you go?'

'I walked down Westwood Road towards the industrial estate.'

'Why did you go that way?'

'I was goin' home.'

The Judge made a sign to an attendant and was brought a map which must have been shown to the court before I came in.

'It's rather a long way round, isn't it?' he asked.

'Well, it makes a walk,' said Walter. There was a hint of defiance in his voice.

'And you passed the warehouse where you worked?' said Mr Goodwin.

'Aye.'

'But you saw nothing wrong?'

'Not then I didn't.'

'When did you?'

'A minute or two afterwards. I'd just stopped to light a fag . . .'

'You lit it with what?' asked the Judge.

'With me lighter,' said Walter. And then the whole court could see the dismay in his face as he realized he'd made a hash of things. For we'd already heard that the lighter had been found at the spot where the fire started.

'I must have dropped the lighter inside when I went in to see if I could put the fire out,' Walter added hurriedly.

'We'll come to that in a minute,' said Mr Goodwin. I thought I detected a despairing note in his voice. But he went on questioning Walter. Walter told him that, knowing where the fire-extinguishers were, he thought he could put the fire out. The heat and smoke were too much for him, he said, and he collapsed. It was thanks to Dick and myself that he was still alive.

Mr Goodwin's last question was: 'Did you set fire to that warehouse?'

Walter drew himself up to his full height, which isn't very great.

'No, sir,' he said in a strong voice.

But the damage had been done. I don't suppose a soul in court believed him.

Mr Rimington began the cross-examination gently. He went once more through Walter's account of what had happened, and I had to admit that he was cleverer than I'd thought at first, because by the time he'd finished it sounded a very unlikely story indeed. And then quite suddenly he went in to the attack.

'I put it to you, Thompson,' he said forcefully, 'that what really happened was this. You set the place on fire, you ran off as fast as you could go, then you remembered you'd left your lighter and you tried to go back for it. That's the truth of the matter, isn't it?' He raised his voice. 'Isn't it?'

Walter stood for a moment white-faced and silent, his lips moving but nothing coming out. And then he lost control of himself.

'Yes, I did it!' he shouted. 'I did it! But it was him that put me up to it! Old Widdershins himself!'

There wasn't a sound in court. Walter looked round him wildly and went on:

'It was all for the insurance. Every time he came into the place he used to say he could do with a good fire. He told me half a dozen times it'd be a good bargain if he was to pay somebody five hundred quid to send the place up in flames. An' then, two or three weeks before it happened, he said the time to have that fire would be the night of the Civic Ball, because he'd be at the ball, an' nobody could say he did it hisself. An' he gave me a look that spoke louder than words. I knew what he meant all right. I wasn't born yesterday. "I could just do with five hundred quid, Mr Widdowson," I said. An' he gives that little smile an' says "Now's your chance, Thompson!" It was all his own doin'. It's him that should be standin' here, me Lord, not me!'

You might have thought that this outburst would have caused a sensation, but it didn't. Everybody seemed to take it quite calmly. In fact the one thing that was obvious was that it wasn't doing Walter any good.

'That will do,' said Mr Rimington coldly. 'Let me get this straight, Thompson. You now admit that you started this fire, although you declared on oath a few minutes ago that you did not. And you ask the jury to believe that Alderman Widdowson, a member of the city council for twenty years

141

and a businessman of unblemished reputation, was bribing you to do so?'

'They won't believe it!' snarled Walter.

'I'm quite sure they won't,' said Mr Rimington. 'The suggestion is preposterous. My Lord, I have no further questions to put.'

'Would you like to re-examine your witness, Mr Goodwin?' asked the Judge.

Mr Goodwin shrugged his shoulders helplessly.

'I think not, my Lord,' he said.

When Walter had returned to the dock, Mr Rimington stood up again and asked for Alderman Widdowson to be recalled to the witness-box.

'Since these allegations have been made,' he said, 'they had better be dealt with. Mr Widdowson, you have heard what the defendant said. He claimed first that you had told him it would be worth your while to pay five hundred pounds to have the warehouse set on fire; secondly that you told him the night of the Civic Ball would be the time to have the fire, since it would be clear that you could not have started it yourself; thirdly that when he said he could just do with five hundred pounds, you replied, "Now's your chance, Thompson." Is there any truth whatever, Mr Widdowson, in any of these allegations?'

Mr Widdowson was perfectly composed.

'There is no truth in them whatever,' he replied in a clear, firm voice. 'They are a tissue of falsehood from beginning to end.'

I was watching Walter's face. I wondered whether there would be another outburst. But Walter seemed to have shot his bolt. His attitude now was dejected, and he didn't even look at Mr Widdowson.

'Thank you, Mr Widdowson,' said Mr Rimington. 'That disposes of that.'

Mr Goodwin was asked if he wanted to cross-examine,

and after a moment's hesitation he said he didn't. No doubt he felt there was little chance of shaking Mr Widdowson. In fact Mr Goodwin looked almost as downcast as Walter, and I could understand it. It was one man's word against another, and I was sure that anyone who'd seen them both in the witness-box would believe Mr Widdowson rather than Walter.

The rest of the trial was something of an anticlimax. Mr Rimington made his final speech for the prosecution in the tones of a man who knew he'd won. He no longer needed, he said, to prove that Walter had started the fire, because Walter now admitted it. Hitherto, he said, the one aspect of the case that had seemed a little surprising was that a man should have been prepared to seek such a drastic revenge for what could only have been a petty grudge. But the jury had now seen what kind of man Walter was, and had seen that he was ready to hurl wild accusations at a leading citizen – accusations that could have no foundation except in sheer malice. He asked the Judge to pass a sentence severe enough to deter anyone else who might be tempted to express his spite in so wicked and disastrous a way.

Mr Goodwin, in his closing speech for the defence, seemed spiritless, and that wasn't surprising. His client had pretty well cut the ground from under his feet. He didn't go so far as to admit that he believed Walter was lying, but all his speech really amounted to was a claim that Walter was a pathetic character rather than a wicked one. The jury retired, and came back in less than five minutes with a verdict of Guilty.

'Before I pass sentence,' said the Judge in that beautiful voice of his, 'I think it proper to make it clear that I do not attach the slightest importance to the allegations which the defendant made against one of the witnesses. The defendant is an admitted liar, having previously stated on oath that he did not start the fire at all. I have formed the impression that he is stupid enough, and malicious enough, to make any allegation that might come into his head. Alderman

143

Widdowson was a most satisfactory and obviously truthful witness. He leaves the court without a stain – without even the shadow of a stain – on his character.'

Then the Judge turned to Walter, and gave him a sound telling-off and a sentence of eighteen months' imprisonment.

16

'I don't know what to think,' said Tony Boyd unhappily. 'I just don't know what to think about it.'

'I always was suspicious of that Widdowson man,' said Dick. 'Now I know.'

'But you don't know,' said Tony. 'That's the whole trouble. You don't know. Nobody knows.'

We were in Tony's study at St Jude's Vicarage, the afternoon of the day after the trial.

'You saw my uncle last night before they took him away,' I said to Tony. 'What did he say then?'

'He said it was all Widdowson's doing,' said Tony. 'He was very bitter.'

'You see?' said Dick.

'But before the trial he was saying all along that he never did the job at all. So what value can you put on Walter Thompson's word?'

'The Judge didn't put any value on it,' I said.

'Nevertheless,' said Tony, 'I know your uncle pretty well by now. He's untruthful, but there are times when I think he's telling the truth. I don't believe he's capable of making up a story like the one he finally told. Also he stuck to it firmly last night after the hearing, even though it hadn't done him any good.'

'Well, if you want to know, it makes me sick!' said Dick. 'Talk about British justice!'

'There was nothing wrong with the trial,' said Tony. 'We've got to face facts. It must have seemed pretty certain to the court that Walter was lying. If I'd been one of the jury I expect I'd have thought so myself. The point is that in spite of overwhelming probability we three aren't satisfied. But it's hard to see what we can do about it.'

'We could tackle Mr Widdowson ourselves,' suggested Dick.

'That's no good, I'm afraid,' said Tony. 'He won't discuss the matter. However, let's just run through the whole thing again and see if we get any ideas. Dick, tell us your theory once more.'

'I think it was a plot to get the insurance money,' said Dick promptly. 'As soon as Widdowson and Brindley knew Walter had been in trouble, they saw he'd make a perfect cat's-paw. They started by getting him into debt. I expect it was Brindley who put him up to selling the furniture when it was still on hire-purchase. Then you played into their hands, Tony, though you didn't realize it, by getting him a job at the warehouse. After that, all they had to do was to keep working on him – making it clear what he had to do without actually putting it into words. And they'd decided from the start that if he got caught they'd leave him in the lurch. It would be his word against Widdowson's, and he wouldn't stand a chance.'

'Well, that's possible,' said Tony. 'Supposing for a moment that you're right, how do we set about proving it?'

The answer was obvious, really. I don't know why Tony or Dick didn't think of it before I did.

'We talk to Mr Brindley!' I said.

Dick's eyes lit up. He slapped me on the back.

'That's the idea!' he said. 'We'll squeeze the truth out of old Brindley!'

Mr Brindley hadn't been a witness at the trial. There was no reason why he should have been. He worked at the shop in Westwood Parade, not at the warehouse, and so far as the court was concerned there was nothing to connect him with Walter or the fire.

'Let's go and see him this minute!' said Dick.

'Don't be carried away,' said Tony. 'This may not lead to anything. But it's worth trying. Ten past five. We might just get to the showroom before they close.'

On the way to Westwood, Dick and I told Tony all we knew about Mr Brindley and his dealings with Walter. We reached the Parade a minute or two after half past five. Mr Brindley's assistant had just left the showroom, and Mr Brindley himself was locking up.

At first he mistook us for customers.

'A little late, gentlemen,' he said. 'A little late. But don't worry, I'm not going to turn you away. Service is our watchword at Widdowson's – an old-fashioned watchword but a sound one. Now, what can I have the pleasure of showing you?'

Then he recognized me, and was startled.

'What do you want?' he said, and made as if to lock the door after all.

'Just a moment, Mr Brindley,' said Tony. He'd drawn himself up to his full height of six feet something, and he spoke in a tone of authority that I'd never heard from him before. 'Just a moment. I'm Anthony Boyd. Kevin and Dick here are friends of mine. And we'd like to have a brief word with you.'

Mr Brindley must have realized that it would be about Walter, and he could have refused to say anything. But perhaps he was nervous about what might happen if he did.

Or perhaps Tony's clerical collar and sheer force of character were too much for him. Anyway, he beckoned us inside, and asked us to sit in a corner of the showroom away from the window, on a sofa and chairs that were for sale. It was the queerest place for an interview you could imagine.

'Well?' he said uneasily.

'Mr Brindley,' said Tony. 'It was through you that Walter Thompson – Kevin's uncle – first became embroiled with the Widdowson organization.'

'We delivered some furniture to his house, yes.'

'And he wanted to send it back.'

'That's correct. But I pointed out that it had been damaged.'

'Nevertheless, the day after you called on him it disappeared,' said Tony.

'I don't know anything about that,' said Mr Brindley quickly.

'I gather that you found out that Thompson had been in trouble, and you spoke to him privately for several minutes. I wonder if you'd care to tell us what that conversation was about?'

'I really can't remember.'

'You were putting him up to selling the stuff, weren't you?' said Dick, interrupting. 'Trying to get a hold over him.'

Tony frowned at Dick. I thought Mr Brindley would protest. Instead he said:

'I remember now. I certainly didn't suggest that he should sell our furniture. On the contrary, knowing him to be of doubtful character, I went out of my way to warn him not to do so. I pointed out that it would be an offence.'

'Negative suggestion, eh?' said Dick, butting in again. 'You put it into his head by telling him not to do it.'

'That'll do, Dick!' said Tony sharply.

147

Mr Brindley was beginning to recover his poise after the shock of being confronted by the three of us.

'I advised Walter Thompson,' he went on in something more like his normal plummy voice, 'to keep the furniture, since we could hardly take it back in its damaged state, and to see how he got on with the payments. I told him that if after a few weeks he found the instalments burdensome, we would see if we could rearrange matters so as to make it easier. And as I heard no more from him, I assumed that he was taking my advice.'

'A few minutes after you saw Thompson, your car was seen parked outside Mr Widdowson's house,' said Tony.

'No doubt it was,' said Mr Brindley easily. 'Mr Widdowson takes a personal interest in our customers, so I went to tell him what I had done. He approved entirely.'

Tony was silent now, but Dick stepped in once more.

'You were at the warehouse one evening in the middle of June,' he said, 'and I heard Mr Widdowson tell you, "I think we've got it all tied up, Joe." I'd like to know what he meant by that.'

'And I'd like to know what you meant by hanging around Mr Widdowson's warehouse,' retorted Mr Brindley. He had got all his usual bounce back by now.

Dick reddened. Mr Brindley didn't wait for an answer.

'I fear you are a most inquisitive and ill-mannered young man,' he said. 'However, as it happens, I remember that evening quite well. I met Mr Widdowson at the warehouse to discuss arrangements for the July sales. When we had finished, I believe he did use words similar to the ones you quote. It seems very natural that he should.'

After pausing a moment for effect, Mr Brindley went on:

'Perhaps now, Mr Boyd, I may be spared any more of this interrogation. You know quite well, of course, that you and your protégés have no right to ask me such questions.'

'I realize that,' said Tony quietly.

'However, you've seen that I have nothing to hide. I can tell you quite plainly that if you imagine you are going to pin something shady on to Mr Widdowson or myself, you are very much mistaken.'

'And that, I suppose, is your last word?' said Tony.

Mr Brindley smiled, and spoke with a kind of insulting politeness.

'I think so, for the present. But some day perhaps I may have the pleasure of a visit from you for a happier purpose – as a customer? I should be delighted to show you our stocks of the latest designs. Any time, Mr Boyd, any time. . .' He smiled again, a smile of victory, as he showed us out.

'The fat slug!' growled Dick, as we got back into Tony's car. 'The fat slug!'

'Well, so much for that,' said Tony. 'No change out of *him*. I'm afraid I'm not too hopeful about your theory, Dick. First, it's all very well talking about "a plot to get the insurance money", but you'd have to prove Mr Widdowson did in fact stand to gain something by the fire.'

'Anne once told me he had a lot of old stock he couldn't sell,' I said.

'A fire would be a drastic kind of stock clearance!' said Tony. 'You'd need a more substantial motive than that. Of course there could be half a dozen reasons why it might pay a man to send his own premises up in smoke – but in this case we don't know of any. Secondly, I think Brindley's probably telling the truth about what he said to Walter. He wouldn't have been so foolish as to tell him in so many words to sell the furniture he'd just bought. If the pair of them did entangle Walter in their plans, you can be sure it was done by hints, gestures, tones of voice – nothing that anybody could put a finger on. As for what you overheard at the warehouse, Dick, let's face it – it might have meant anything or nothing. As evidence it's worthless.'

'I still think the whole thing was a plot,' declared Dick stoutly. 'Walter Thompson was the fall-guy.'

'You may be right,' said Tony. 'You may well be right. But we'll never prove it. We haven't the resources. So far as the police are concerned, the case is closed, and I don't think for a moment it'll be reopened.'

Dick sighed heavily, but said nothing.

'Now there are two more possibilities,' said Tony. 'One is that Mr Widdowson is a perfectly honest, decent man, who tried to help Walter and merely succeeded in bringing all this trouble on himself. It could be that every word he said in court was true.'

'I don't believe it,' said Dick.

I heard in memory the voice of Anne Widdowson: 'My dad's great . . . he does a lot of good.' Not for the first time, I wondered if all our suspicions had been fanciful nonsense.

'Then there's a third possibility,' said Tony, 'and it's the one I'm inclined to accept. As I said, I don't think Walter could have invented his story. I think it may well be that Mr Widdowson wasn't unwilling to have his warehouse burned down. I think he may well have dropped hints to Walter to that effect. I think he may not have known himself whether he was really serious, or only half serious, or a quarter serious. And when it was all over, he may have persuaded himself that he was never serious at all.'

'You mean . . .?' I said.

'I mean, to sum the whole thing up, that Mr Widdowson may have been, as Dick believes, a hundred per cent guilty, or he may have been, as the court thought, a hundred per cent innocent. But he may also have been, as I'm inclined to think, somewhere in between. Nobody knows the full truth – perhaps not even himself.'

I was baffled.

'But, Tony,' I said, 'surely a thing's either true or false, and a person's either honest or dishonest.'

Tony smiled wryly.

'Life's not so simple as that,' he said. 'There's no telling exactly what makes people tick. We don't even understand ourselves, never mind other people.'

'I understand old Widdershins,' said Dick fiercely, 'and he's a crook!'

'Maybe,' said Tony. 'The fact is that it's a mystery. Not a neat, tidy mystery to be unravelled in the last chapter of a book, but a rather murky mystery that we can't solve. Not a matter of black and white, but of shades of grey.'

Dick and I were silent for a long time. I was brooding over Tony's words. And when at last Dick spoke, it was in a more thoughtful tone than I'd ever heard from him in his life before.

'All right, Tony,' he said. 'You win. We don't really know who's guilty, and we probably never will. We only know who's got the blame. That's Walter. And we know who suffers. That's Doris and Kevin and Sandra and Harold and Jean.'

'We'll get by,' I said. For I'd had time to think what I was going to do. I'd already made a decision about my own future. And – together with Sandra – I'd made a decision about Harold's.

17

'Anne!' I called. 'Anne!'

It was a fortnight later. She was coming down the steps of Westwood Library. I thought she'd seen me, but she looked the other way, so perhaps she hadn't.

'Anne!' I called, a little louder.

I decided that if she didn't respond I'd give it up. But now she looked round.

'Hello, Kevin,' she said, without smiling.

'Anne, I wanted to see you. Sit here on the wall a minute.'

'What did you want to see me for? It's no good.'

'We can still be friends, can't we?'

'I didn't know we *were* friends. I've met you two or three times, that's all.'

Most times I couldn't have kept on in the face of a snub like that. But I was full of desperate courage. I didn't want to give up my acquaintance with Anne.

'I think we were friends,' I said. 'It doesn't matter all that much how long you've known somebody. Being friends is a kind of sympathy between people – either it's there or it isn't. I think it was there between us.'

She softened a little.

'You mean that time on the lake,' she said. 'Yes, we were friends. I felt it too.'

'Does it have to be "were", not "are"?'

'But, Kevin!' said Anne. She was silent for a moment. Then, with passion:

'It's your uncle! Saying those dreadful things about my father! It was reported in all the papers, with great big headlines. I know the Judge said it was lies, but there'll always be people who think there must be something in it. You can't throw mud without some of it sticking. It makes me feel – oh, I don't know – it makes me feel dirty.'

'It doesn't reflect on you,' I said.

'It does! It reflects on my father, and I feel it just as if it was me. And life's been so horrible lately. The insurance company have been snooping round and asking him all kinds of questions. He says they're satisfied now, but it isn't nice to have that kind of thing going on. What with that and the trial, he's had weeks of dreadful worry. Oh, Kevin, it was wicked!'

152

'Listen, Anne,' I said, 'I honestly don't know what the rights and wrongs of this thing are – '

'I do!' she said coldly.

'What I wanted to say to you,' I went on, 'is that it's between your father and my uncle, it isn't between you and me.'

'It *is* between you and me. You don't understand. Boys never understand. Don't you see, Kevin, it's impossible. If we were to stay friends, it would always be there in the background. And what would my father say?'

'Do you only have the friends your father approves of?' I asked bitterly.

'No, I don't. But if you mean, does it matter to me what my father thinks, yes it does!'

'All right,' I said. This was hurting badly. I must have looked pretty sick. I started to get up from the wall, but she put her hand on mine to stop me. It was the only time she ever touched me. Her hand was a good one – not dainty, but brown and strong. For a moment I felt the sympathy flow between us again.

'Kevin, I know it must all have been awful for you. And I know you're not to blame for anything. You're nice.'

'Thank you,' I said with a touch of sarcasm.

'But it won't do. You know it won't, really.'

'And what happens when we meet in the street?' I asked. 'Are you going to look straight through me, or what?'

'No, of course not. I shall say, "Hello, Kevin", and you'll say, "Hello, Anne". But let's just leave it at that. Please.'

I didn't want to leave it at that. I knew she was wrong. But I couldn't think of a way to deal with the situation. We didn't even say good-bye. She just walked off one way along the street and I went the other.

18

It was September, and the trees were changing colour. People who'd been away were back from holiday now. The local schools had started again. In Widdershins Crescent the last houses were finished, and occupied too. The road had been made up. There were no more workmen about, but people seemed to be busier than ever in their gardens. The whole place was taking shape. Instead of the raw look it had had when we moved in, the Crescent seemed neat and clean and permanent. It was dull, perhaps, compared with the Jungle – I still had moments of homesickness for the sloping streets and the alleyways and the tangle of derelict buildings down by the canal bank – but it was a decent place to live.

Six weeks ago I'd left school for good, and got a job at the new supermarket on the Parade. Sandra had said her piece against it, and Tony had said his, and Sheila had said hers, and they'd even had Mr Reed, the headmaster, come and speak to me, but I'd left school after all. Well, I had to. It was the only way we could manage. And it wasn't a bad job. All I had to do was load the shelves and stamp the price-tickets.

The great day in our household was Tuesday, September the fifteenth. I ought to have been at work by eight, but I'd fixed things so I could be late. And you never saw such a sight as Widdershins Crescent that morning. All the people who weren't at work were at their garden gates, or gossiping in little groups, and there was a great air of excitement. You'd have thought the Queen was coming.

But it wasn't royalty they were expecting. It was Harold.

On the dot of half past eight he appeared on the front doorstep. He was a dapper little figure. Well-fitting navy-blue jacket, well-creased grey trousers, new navy raincoat folded over his arm, new leather brief-case in his hand. Sandra had worked her fingers to the bone to fit him out, but even so he'd needed a lot of things that had to be paid for. And without being asked, without even a grumble, the people of Widdershins Crescent had paid.

A photographer stopped him for a doorstep picture. It wasn't any of the photographers from the national Press who'd crowded round our doorstep a few weeks ago when Walter and Dick and I were all heroes. It was just Ted Bingham from the *Westwood Advertiser*. Still, the *Advertiser* represented real everyday life where real everyday things happened to people you knew. It counted more to us than the far-off glamorous world of the nationals. And Ted was having a good innings. He took pictures of Harold being kissed by Doris and then by Sandra. Then Harold advanced as far as the garden gate, and Ted photographed him again, surrounded by admirers like a film-star and with a dozen hands all stretching forward to shake his.

Then somebody started a panic that Harold would be missing his bus, so the crowd dropped back, and Ted put his equipment away, and Harold strode along the street with his shoulders squared and his head held high. He was having a great time, the little wretch. And people still kept bobbing out with last-minute presents or exhortations. Harold got a pen from Mrs Slater, a pencil-box from old Mrs Brittain (his third, if she'd only known), some drawing-instruments from Mr Farrow, tenpenny and fifty-penny pieces from several other people. He disappeared at last round the corner into Westwood Road, accompanied by a sort of send-off committee who meant to cheer him on to the bus.

I suppose nobody in Widdershins Crescent has had anything special in the way of education, and none of their children have done anything striking either. But they were all proud of Harold. Whatever anyone might have thought about privileged schools that most children couldn't go to, nobody grudged him his triumph. He was a credit to the street. He was also, I realized, a sign that in spite of everything we were beginning to belong.

A thin cheer came from the bus stop, and I knew that Harold had gone. He'd be back at teatime, of course, but by then a new age would have begun. It was an old fantasy of Harold's that one day he would be Sir Harold Thompson, the world-famous scientist. Well, you never knew. It wasn't impossible.

I'd borrowed Dick's bicycle to go to and from the store, but this morning I walked with Sandra as far as Westwood Road, where she had to catch the bus for her own school a few minutes later. I looked sideways at Sandra as I wheeled the bike along beside her. She was still the same Sandra, thin and upright, with sharp determined face and straight fair hair. I wondered if she was beginning to look pretty. Perhaps not, I thought, perhaps not, but I liked her as she was, and so did Dick. And I had the feeling that I get from time to time of a special bond with Sandra. We have always stood by each other and seen things through.

Then I saw a small elderly car parked in Westwood Road. That was like Tony Boyd's car. In fact it *was* Tony Boyd's car. Tony waved, and Sandra and I waved back and ran up to him. Sheila, slim again now, was with him, and the baby too, in a carry-cot. Sandra clucked over it and stroked its cheeks with her forefinger.

'What are you doing here, Tony?' I asked.

'I thought I'd take Harold to school, seeing it was his first day.'

'But you haven't done.'

'No, I didn't want to spoil the show. They were all having

156

such fun seeing him on to the bus, and he seemed to be enjoying himself. It might have looked as if I was taking him away from them.'

That's just like Tony. He is always worrying over other people's feelings.

'Anyway, Harold's a credit to both of you,' Tony went on. 'Specially to you, Sandra.'

'I only did what I had to do,' said Sandra defensively. 'Anyone'd've done the same.' And then, as if she were being criticized rather than praised:

'Well, the lad's got to have his chance, hasn't he? We can't all be as clever as our Harold. It wouldn't do to waste it.'

'I've missed giving Harold a lift,' said Tony, 'but, Sandra, I can give you one, can't I? I suppose you're on your way to school? Hop in.'

'There'll be a bus in a minute,' said Sandra.

'Don't argue. Get in.'

This is not normally the way to make Sandra do anything, but she stepped meekly into the car. And before Tony drove off he beckoned me across.

'Let me tell you something, Kevin,' he said. 'You've won. Don't ever forget that. You've won.'

'What do you mean, Tony?' I asked. But Tony wasn't going to explain himself. He let in the clutch and the car moved away. Sheila and Sandra waved from the back window.

I pushed the bicycle out from the kerb and punted it along for a few paces. I was on my way to work. There'd be a wage packet at the week-end. With any luck I'd have a bike of my own before too long. I'd all my life in front of me, and there were all kinds of interesting things to do.

I swung my leg over. The bicycle gathered speed on the slope down Westwood Hill. I didn't have to pedal. It just

157

floated along. Or perhaps it was more like flying. I started to whistle.

We'd won. Tony said we'd won. I didn't know what we'd won, but I felt like a winner. I whistled, louder and louder. We'd won.

Heard about the Puffin Club?

. . . it's a way of finding out more about Puffin
books and authors, of winning prizes (in
competitions), sharing jokes, a secret code, and
perhaps seeing your name in print! When you
join you get a copy of our magazine, *Puffin
Post*, sent to you four times a year, a badge and
a membership book.

For details of subscription and an application
form, send a stamped addressed envelope to:

The Puffin Club Dept A
Penguin Books Limited
Bath Road
Harmondsworth
Middlesex UB7 0DA

and if you live in Australia, please write to:

The Australian Puffin Club
Penguin Books Australia Limited
P.O. Box 257
Ringwood
Victoria 3134